FOR EXTRA FRIGHTS, STAY OVERNIGHT!

Your Stay Includes:

Comfortable Beds of Nails

Slime-ing Pool

Daily Housecreeping

STAGGER INN

VACANCY

Call ahead—
people are dying to get in.

Check In: 4:00 p.m.
Check Out: No one has yet!

Don't forget to stop by our Gift Chop!

www.EnterHorrorLand.com

FOR EXTRA FRIGHTS,
STAY OVERNIGHT!
ESCAPE
HORRORLAND
STAGGER INN
Your Stay Includes:
Call ahead—
Check In: 4:00 p.m.
Check Out: No one has yet!
Don't forget to stop by our Gift Chop!
www.EnterHorrorLand.com

REVENGE OF THE LIVING DUMMY

R.L. STINE

SCHOLASTIC INC.
New York Toronto London Auckland Sydney
Mexico City New Delhi Hong Kong Buenos Aires

GOOSEBUMPS HorrorLand™

GOOSEBUMPS® MOST WANTED

GOOSEBUMPS®
Also available as ebooks

ISBN-13: 978-0-439-91869-5

Goosebumps book series created by Parachute Press, Inc.

Goosebumps HorrorLand #1: *Revenge of the Living Dummy*
copyright © 2008 by Scholastic Inc.

32 31 30 29   16/0

Printed in the U.S.A.
First printing, April 2008

3 RIDES IN 1!

REVENGE OF
THE LIVING DUMMY

1

You may wonder why my best friend, Molly Molloy, and I were in the old graveyard late at night.

I shivered as I thought about what we were doing. Wind howled through the trees, and pale streaks of lightning cracked the sky.

"Hurry, Molly," I whispered, hugging myself as the moon disappeared behind the clouds. "It's going to storm."

"I *am* hurrying, Britney," Molly said. "But the ground . . . it's really hard."

We were digging a grave. We took turns. One of us shoveled while the other stood lookout.

I felt cold raindrops on my forehead. I kept my eyes on the low picket fence near the street. Nothing moved. The only sounds were the *scrape* of the shovel in the dirt and a drumroll of thunder, deep but far away.

Across from me, an old gravestone made a creaking sound as it tilted in the wind.

I sucked in my breath. I suddenly pictured the old stone toppling over. And someone *crawling out* from the grave beneath it.

Okay, okay. I have a wild imagination. Everyone knows that about me.

My mom says I'll either be a writer or a crazy person.

She thinks that's really funny.

Sometimes having a strong imagination is a good thing. And sometimes it just makes things more scary.

Like tonight.

Molly stopped shoveling to push the hair out of her eyes. Raindrops pattered on the blanket of dead leaves on the ground. "Britney, does this look deep enough?" she asked in a hoarse whisper.

I glanced at the glass coffin on the ground. "Keep digging. We have to totally cover it," I said.

I turned back to the street. It was late, and the neighborhood stood dark and still. But what if someone drove by and saw us?

How could we ever explain the grave we were digging?

How could we explain why we were there?

Molly groaned and dug the shovel blade into the dirt.

The dead leaves crackled. I held my breath and listened. Footsteps. Someone creeping quickly through the leaves toward us.

"Molly —" I whispered.

Then I saw them, huddled low, moving in a line. Raccoons. A pack of them, little eyes glowing. The black fur on their faces made the little creatures look like they were wearing masks.

They froze when they saw us. And then stood up taller.

Do raccoons ever attack?

These raccoons looked really hungry. I imagined them stampeding Molly and me. Swarming over us, clawing and biting.

A bright flash of lightning brought them into clear focus. They were staring at the little glass coffin. Did they think there was food inside?

A clap of thunder — closer now — startled them. The leader turned and scuttled away over the leaves. The others followed.

I shivered and wiped rain off my forehead.

Molly handed me the shovel. "Your turn," she said. "It's almost finished."

The wooden handle scratched my hand. I kicked dirt off the blade and stepped up to the shallow hole. "No one will ever find it here," I said. "Once we bury the evil thing, we'll be safe from it."

Molly didn't answer.

I had the sudden feeling something was wrong.

I turned and saw Molly staring with her mouth open. Staring at the tall gravestone next to us. She pointed. "Brit —"

And then I heard the old stone creak. And saw the pale hand slowly reach out from the grave.

No time to move. No time to scream.

I stood frozen — and watched the hand wrap its cold, bony fingers around my ankle.

And *then* I started to scream.

Two weeks earlier, I had other things on my mind. I wasn't thinking about the old graveyard down the street. I had other problems.

Well, one *big* problem. And his name was Ethan.

Ethan is my cousin, and it isn't nice to hate your cousin. So let's just say he isn't one of my favorite people on this planet.

I like to make lists. And if I made a list of My Top 5,000 Favorite People in the World, my cousin Ethan wouldn't be on it.

Get what I'm saying?

It was almost dinnertime on a Friday night. And I was perched on the edge of the bed in my new bedroom.

Why did I have a new bedroom?

Because Mom and Dad kicked me out of my awesome room in the attic to make room for guess who — Ethan. So now I had to sleep in Mom's sewing room. And the sewing machine was still against the wall. So how much room did I have? Try *not much*.

I was talking on my cell to Molly. Molly is maybe the only person who understands what a pain Ethan is. Because she's met him. And she had two bruised knees to prove it.

Whoever told Ethan that kicking people is funny?

Molly and I are like sisters. If you mention Molly Molloy, you have to mention me, Britney Crosby, too. We are both twelve, and we live on the same block, and we've always been in the same class since third grade.

We both like to draw and paint. We both like to make lists of everything. We are always finishing each other's sentences — like we have one brain!

Molly is a little taller than me and more into sports. We both have coppery hair, although hers is lighter and curlier. And we both have brown eyes.

I'm the funny one. It's hard to make Molly laugh.

I think she's more serious than me because her parents split up, and she lives with her dad. He travels a lot, and he's kind of a flake. So she feels like she has to be the grown-up in the house.

Obviously, I've thought about it a lot.

I once made a list of my good qualities and my bad qualities. And one of my good qualities is that I really try to understand my friends.

"I can't come over now," I told Molly. "That brat Ethan will be here any minute. Dad went to the bus station to pick him up."

Molly groaned into the phone. "Maybe you'll get lucky. Maybe he missed the bus. Why is he coming to stay with you anyway?"

"His parents had to go away or something," I said. "He's even coming to our school. I think he's in third grade."

"He's such a sicko," Molly said. "Maybe you should move over here till he leaves."

I rolled my eyes. "Like my mom would go for that."

"She knows you hate him," Molly said.

"I'm supposed to feel sorry for Ethan because he's had such a tough life," I said. "You know. His parents were both sick for a long time and didn't pay any attention to him."

Molly shook her head. "Yeah. I remember."

I groaned. "So Mom and Dad say I have to take good care of him. Every ten minutes, they remind me I have to be nice to him."

"Hel-lo!" Molly said. "Do they know he kicks people when the grown-ups aren't looking? Do they know how he kept trying to trip you and make you fall down the stairs? Did you tell them he tricked you into eating a sandwich that had dead bugs in it?"

"He's totally bratty, but they don't believe me," I said. "Last time Ethan stayed here, he started messing with my computer — and he deleted my whole term paper. He said it was an accident. Then he burst out laughing."

Molly groaned again. "What a creep."

"Molly, what am I going to do?" I wailed. "He's coming to live with us for *weeks*."

Molly was silent for a moment. Then she said softly, "Face it, Britney. Your life is over."

"OHHHH!" I let out a cry as I heard a deafening *crash*. From downstairs?

I nearly dropped the phone.

Was Ethan here already?

I hurried into the kitchen — and saw Mom bent over, picking pieces of china off the floor.

"I can't believe I dropped that plate," she said, shaking her head.

Mom has short, dark brown hair with a streak of white in the front. She is small and skinny and totally high energy. And she's kind of pretty, except her black-framed glasses make her look like a philosophy professor or something.

She's always in a hurry, and she always drops things. And then she says, "I can't believe I dropped that."

"Maybe you're nervous about Ethan," I said, bending to pick up a jagged piece of china. "I know I am."

"Hey." She pinched my cheek. I don't think she meant to hurt me, but she pinched too hard. I'm the only person in the world she pinches. I don't really get it.

"Good attitude — remember?" she said. "Good attitude at all times. You promised."

"I had my fingers crossed," I said.

How *could* I have a good attitude?

The last time Ethan visited, we got into an actual fistfight. Can you imagine? Quiet little Britney Crosby giving her cousin a bloody nose and making him cry in front of all her friends?

That's not like me at all. But he just makes me *crazy!*

"Give Ethan a chance," Mom said, brushing off the front of her jeans. She wears tight designer jeans, and she looks pretty good in them. She's so small, we can almost share clothes. Weird.

"He's had a lot of problems," Mom said. "And now his parents have left him for who knows how long. He's not bad. He just acts out because he's lonely."

Yeah. Right.

I heard a car door slam. Then Dad's voice in the garage.

"They're here," Mom said. "Remember, Britney, you've got to be the grown-up in this situation. Get off to a good start with Ethan, and everything will be fine."

"I'm going to try. Really," I said, and I meant it.

The door from the garage swung open. Dad stepped into the kitchen, carrying Ethan's two suitcases. "Our new family member has arrived," he said.

Ethan came bouncing in behind him, a big grin on his face. Ethan looks like a sweet little boy. He is short and pale and very blond. He has bright blue eyes and a cute, pointed little chin. He wore a gray hoodie over baggy jeans.

And what was that *thing* slumped over his shoulder?

I squinted at it. A grinning ventriloquist's dummy.

"Hi, Aunt Roz," Ethan said.

Mom shook a finger at the dummy. "Ethan — what is *that*?"

He pulled the dummy off his shoulder and held it up. It had an ugly face with painted blue eyes, a chipped lower lip, and an awful grin.

"This is Mr. Badboy," Ethan said. "Mr. Badboy is my best friend."

Totally pitiful, I thought.

But I put a smile on my face and said, "Hey, Ethan."

Ethan came running over to me, holding the dummy in front of him.

"Mr. Badboy," he said, "say hi to my cousin Britney."

I saw it coming, but I couldn't move in time.

The dummy's wooden hand swung up fast — then came down hard. And — *CLONNNNK* — slammed me in the forehead.

"Whooooa." A sharp pain shot through my head. I pressed my hands against my throbbing temples, trying to push the pain away.

"Be careful with that thing," Dad scolded Ethan.

"It wasn't my fault!" Ethan cried, backing away from me. "Mr. Badboy did it."

Here we go again, I thought.

Ethan moved the dummy's mouth up and down. *"I'm a BAAAAAAD boy!"* the dummy said in a shrill baby voice.

Mom turned and hurried to the fridge. "We'd better put some ice on it, Brit," she said. "You're gonna have a bump."

I glared at Ethan. Was it an accident?

"Sometimes Mr. Badboy doesn't know his own strength," Ethan said.

"Ethan, how about saying you're sorry?" Dad said.

"Mr. Badboy is very sorry," Ethan said.

I pushed past him and headed to the door. "Forget the ice," I said, rubbing my forehead. "I'm going over to Molly's."

Mom hurried after me. She stopped me in the front hall. "Take Ethan with you," she said in a whisper.

"Mom, please — no," I said.

Mom put both hands on my shoulders and narrowed her eyes at me through her glasses. "Britney, he just got here. Don't be rude. Remember what I said about getting off to a good start?"

"He already gave me a *bruise*!" I cried.

But I could see she meant business. I sighed. "Okay. Okay."

I saw Ethan near the kitchen door, and I called to him. "Want to come over to Molly's?"

"Excellent!" Ethan replied. "I'll bring Mr. Badboy."

Thrills, I thought.

We stepped out into a cool, windy evening. The sun had started to dip behind the trees, sending long shadows across the grass.

Molly lives three houses down on the other side of the street. A short walk, but Ethan kept dancing around me, sticking his foot out, trying to trip me.

"Give me a break," I pleaded.

He just giggled in reply. He has a phony hyena giggle that could drive anyone crazy.

I rang the bell and a few seconds later, Molly

15

came to the door. She was wearing faded jeans and a yellow T-shirt with the words MUMBA RULES! in red across the front.

Her dad always brings her T-shirts from the weird places he visits. Don't ask me where on earth Mumba is!

She let out a groan when she saw Ethan.

"Shake hands with Mr. Badboy," Ethan told her. He stuck out the dummy's wooden hand. "Mr. Badboy, this is Molly, Britney's geeky friend."

Nice?

Molly frowned at the dummy and said, "He's almost as ugly as you are, Ethan."

Good one! I laughed and slapped her a high five.

"I'm a BAAAAAAD boy!" the dummy said.

"Perfect," Molly muttered. She led us down the hall to her room. "Dad just got back this morning from one of his crazy trips," she said. "Mumba. It's an island. He's totally pumped. I guess he found some strange dolls there."

Professor Molloy is kind of famous. He works for museums. He says he's a folklore expert. He travels all over the world and brings back ugly, evil-looking dolls, and ancient toys, and voodoo stuff, and skulls and things.

He keeps some of it on display up in his attic. He calls it his Museum of the Weird. He always wants to show it off. But Molly and I don't like to go up there. It totally creeps us out.

16

Ethan put his mouth to my ear and burped really loudly.

I jerked away from him. "Ethan, that's not funny!"

He giggled. "It's a riot!"

We turned the corner to Molly's room — and bumped into Mr. Molloy.

He's big and tall, with a big belly that hangs over his pants. He always wears baggy khakis that are all wrinkled and stained, and sloppy white shirts.

His dark brown hair is long and wild. He has a great smile, a big booming laugh that shakes his belly, and deep blue eyes that just stare — they don't blink — when you talk to him.

He likes to sing in a funny, deep voice. And he's always trying to scare Molly and me with his weird stories.

My dad calls him Wild Man Molloy.

He said hi to me, then turned his gaze on Ethan. "I remember you," he said. "Britney's cousin. And what do we have here?"

He lifted Mr. Badboy off Ethan's shoulder and held the dummy up to study it. "Interesting . . . interesting . . ."

Mr. Molloy examined the wooden head carefully. He ran his finger over the chipped bottom lip. Then he reached a hand beneath Mr. Badboy's shirt and made the mouth snap up and down.

"Interesting dummy," he said. "Ethan, where did this guy come from?"

Ethan shrugged. "My dad found him. I don't know where. I named him Mr. Badboy. Because he's a really bad dude."

Mr. Molloy chuckled. "Interesting." He rubbed his hand over the dummy's painted brown hair. "Why does it look so familiar? Hmmm . . . I could swear I've seen this dummy somewhere before."

He handed Mr. Badboy back to Ethan. "I have some books on ventriloquism. Maybe you'd like to borrow one."

"I don't have to talk for him," Ethan said. "Mr. Badboy talks for himself."

Molly and I looked at each other. We both rolled our eyes. "Yeah. Sure," I muttered.

"Come upstairs," Mr. Molloy said. "I've got something very interesting to show you guys. Something I just brought back from Mumba."

"Maybe later, Dad," Molly said. "We don't really want —"

Mr. Molloy tugged Molly toward the stairs. "Come on up to the attic. You won't be sorry," he said with a wide, devilish grin. "You want to stare into the face of *pure evil* — don't you?"

Ethan's eyes flashed with excitement. "Cool!" he said.

We followed Mr. Molloy up to his attic museum. The stairs were narrow and steep and creaked and groaned under our footsteps.

Whenever I come up here, I feel as if I'm stepping into a haunted house. For one thing, it's very dark and shadowy. Mr. Molloy says that bright light will damage some of his displays.

He keeps everything in glass showcases. It's all so creepy and weird. As you walk past the glass cases, dozens of eyes stare out at you.

"Cool! Check this out!" Ethan cried. He pointed to a case. I squinted in the dim light. Six snake heads, their jaws wide open! Disgusting.

Mr. Molloy stepped up beside Ethan. "Those snake heads were used for gambling," he said. "Just like dice. You hold them between your hands and shake them, then toss them onto the floor. Want to try it?"

"No thanks," Molly said quickly. She pulled her dad away.

Ethan looked disappointed. He held Mr. Badboy up and showed him the snake heads.

A long, skinny animal skull with two rows of pointed teeth grinned at me from the next case. I hurried past it — and the next case, too. It contained two little blue dolls with long blond hair. Their faces were all twisted as if they were crying.

In the next case — a pile of black fur. I looked closer. No. A stuffed animal. With a tiny mouse caught between its curled fangs.

Molly says the attic gives her bad dreams. I don't know how she can fall asleep downstairs knowing that all these horrible creatures are right above her head!

"Over here, guys!" Mr. Molloy called. "Here's the new one you've *got* to check out."

The three of us stepped around the case and gazed down through the glass.

"Ohh, sick," I moaned. I felt my stomach lurch.

"Totally sick," Molly murmured.

"Is that a *real* shrunken head?" Ethan asked.

Mr. Molloy nodded. "I've never seen anything like it in all my travels," he said. "Its body is carved of wood, and it has an actual human head attached to the shoulders."

I took a deep breath and gazed down at it. It was about twelve inches tall. The face was shriveled like an old prune and was a vomit-green color. There were tiny slits where the eyes had once been. Thin wisps of black hair stood straight up from its scalp.

"Awesome!" Ethan said. "Can I hold it?"

"I don't think so," Mr. Molloy replied. "When I tell you the story of this doll, I don't think you'll *want* to come anywhere near it." He chuckled as if he'd just told a good joke.

"Dad, this is really gross," Molly said, shaking her head. She turned her back to the case. "You're not going to keep it here — are you?"

"Let me tell you the story," Mr. Molloy said. "The doll is called a Mind Stealer. The legend goes that if you touch it, you are doomed. Its eyes will open and glow. You will hear a loud, painful buzz. And it will steal your mind right out of your head."

My mouth suddenly felt dry. I wanted to stop staring at the ugly thing, but I couldn't take my eyes off it.

"They say the doll has already claimed twenty minds," Mr. Molloy said. "Twenty poor victims who were left brainless, empty blanks."

I felt a chill run down the back of my neck.

Ethan giggled, but I could tell he was frightened, too.

Molly kept her back to the display case. She tossed her coppery hair back over her shoulder. "Can we go now?" she asked.

I couldn't help myself. I leaned down to get a closer look at the doll.

I stared at the tiny, shriveled head. It was a little smaller than a softball. But it had once been alive. It had once been a *live* human being.

Was it a man or a woman?

I lowered my face to the glass. And let out a cry as the doll whispered, *"How about a kiss, babe?"*

Startled, I stumbled back and nearly knocked Molly over.

Mr. Molloy laughed. "Good one, Ethan!" he said.

Ethan grinned at me. "I'm a pretty good ventriloquist," he said. "I gotcha, Britney." He did a fast tap dance and ended it by stomping hard on my foot.

"Ethan, you're *so* not funny!" I cried. I could feel my face turning hot. I knew I was blushing. How embarrassing to fall for that trick!

Molly turned to her dad. "Do you really believe that mind-stealing stuff?" she asked.

He scratched his head. "I take all these legends seriously," he said. "The legends tell a lot about people and their beliefs."

"Yes or no?" Molly asked. "Do you think it can steal minds or not?"

Her dad was silent for a moment. Then he said, "Yes, I guess I do believe it."

Molly's mouth dropped open. "Dad, if you believe this awful doll is so dangerous, how can you keep it in our house?"

"It's under triple-thick glass," Mr. Molloy replied. "That should make it safe."

"But, Dad —"

"I'm still studying it," he told her. "I've got a call in to some experts. There are people who know a lot more about the doll than I do. I'm waiting to hear from them. In the meantime, I believe the triple-thick glass will make sure that —"

Before he could finish, that brat Ethan cried, "Britney, you're blocking my view!" And he bumped me hard from behind — *into the doll case*!

As my forehead hit the glass, I saw the doll bounce.

Then I heard a loud *BUZZ*.

I gasped. "Oh, no! My *mind*!"

7

Whoa. Wait. I heard the buzz again.

My brain whirred. It took me so long to realize the doll wasn't buzzing. The sound came from my cell phone.

I let out a sigh of relief. It was only my wild imagination going berserk again.

I pulled the phone from my pocket and flipped it open. A text message. From my mom. DINNER ALMOST READY. COME HOME SOON.

I told Molly and Mr. Molloy we had to leave. Ethan started whining that he didn't want to go. He wanted to stay and check out the other weird dolls and objects. But I was happy to get out of there.

The Mind Stealer doll was too creepy to think about. And Mr. Molloy admitted he didn't even know if it was safe to keep it in the house! I knew I'd have nightmares about it.

When we got home, Mom was going crazy in the kitchen, with two pots steaming on the stove and a chicken roasting in the oven. She blew a strand of hair off her forehead and smiled at Ethan.

"I'm making my famous roast chicken in honor of your arrival tonight," she said. "Not quite ready."

She turned to me. "Why don't you go up to Ethan's room and bring down the rest of your junk?"

Ethan gave me a hard tug that almost knocked me over. "Come upstairs, Fat Face. I want to show you my comedy act with Mr. Badboy."

"Fat Face?" I cried. "Don't call me Fat Face, Butt Breath!"

He giggled.

"Stop it," Mom said. She lifted a pot lid and ducked back as steam poured up. "Name-calling isn't funny."

"Yeah. Right. Don't call names, you moron!" Ethan said to me. He tried to jam his elbow into my ribs, but I dodged away.

"Please — go upstairs," Mom said. "Let Ethan show you his comedy act."

"Mom, give me a break," I moaned. "That dummy is so totally lame."

Mom dropped the lid back on the pot and pulled me to the kitchen door. "Go up there with him, Brit. He wants to share something with you. That's a *good* thing."

"But, Mom —"

"And don't make fun of the dummy," she

whispered. "Poor Ethan obviously needs a friend to talk to. So he made one up. Go up to his room and be nice to him."

I let out an exasperated sigh. But then I forced a smile to my face. "Okay, Ethan," I said. "Let's do it."

He let out a cheer and went running up the attic stairs. The dummy's wooden head clonked on each stair as Ethan dragged it by the arm.

I glanced around the attic. My old room. I missed it already.

The room was long and narrow with bright yellow walls. Some of my posters were still hanging up. My desk stood in front of the window between two twin beds, where Molly and I had spent many sleepovers.

No room for sleepovers now, I thought, *in my tiny sewing room*. And then I scolded myself: *Don't be bitter, Brit. You'll get your room back when he leaves.*

Ethan pulled out the desk chair and sat down on it. He set Mr. Badboy on his lap. I dropped to the floor, settled onto the white shag carpet, and leaned my back against the wall.

"Don't laugh too hard," Ethan said. "You'll hurt yourself."

"No problem," I said.

"If you need me to explain any of the jokes, just let me know," he said.

I rolled my eyes. "Just do your act — okay?"

27

Mr. Badboy grinned at me. His eyes opened wide. He had such an ugly smile. Totally evil.

"Britney, is that your face, or did you forget to take out the garbage?" the dummy said. His voice was a shrill rasp.

"Be nice," Ethan scolded the dummy. "That's my cousin."

The dummy leaned toward me. "Britney, something just reminded me of the banana I had for breakfast. Oh, yeah. Your nose!"

The dummy tossed back its head and let out a long donkey laugh. "I'm a BAAAAAAD boy!"

"Is this your act?" I asked Ethan.

He shook his head. "Sometimes Mr. Badboy doesn't cooperate."

"Yeah, right," I muttered.

"Be good," Ethan scolded the dummy.

"I like your long hair," Mr. Badboy said to me. "Too bad it's all growing on your *back*!"

I burst out laughing. The joke was terrible. But Ethan was a really good ventriloquist. I couldn't see his lips move at all.

"Mr. Badboy, please —" Ethan pleaded. "Be nice to Britney."

The dummy's eyes stared into mine. "I know we've just met," he said in his harsh, raspy voice. "But I'm a very romantic dude. And I have three little words I'm dying to say to you."

"Three little words?" I asked.

Mr. Badboy nodded. "Yeah. *Take a bath!*"

I couldn't help myself. I laughed again. I have to admit — I love rude jokes. I guess maybe it's because I'm always so nice.

"Is that your face?" Mr. Badboy asked. "Or are you standing on your head?"

I groaned.

"Don't blame me for these jokes," Ethan replied. "Blame Mr. Badboy."

He turned to the dummy. "You're not very nice," he told it.

"Then stop putting words in my mouth!" Mr. Badboy said.

That made me laugh, too.

"I'm a BAAAAAAD boy!" Mr. Badboy exclaimed.

"You're an *awesome* ventriloquist," I told Ethan. "How did you learn to do that?"

Ethan set Mr. Badboy down on the bed and walked over to me. He shrugged. "I don't know. Just practice, I guess."

I slapped Ethan a high five. "Well, good work, dude. I really think you're talented."

And then I gasped. Because across the room, Mr. Badboy turned his head to me — and opened his mouth in an ugly laugh.

"How did you do that?" I cried.

Ethan's smile faded. "I didn't do it," he said. He took his hand out of his pocket and pointed to Mr. Badboy. "*He* did."

I frowned at him. "Can't you ever be serious?"

"I *am* serious," he insisted.

I was trying to be nice to Ethan, but he always had to act like a jerk. I decided to give it one more try.

"You know, everyone in my school has to do one hour of public service," I said.

"That bites," Ethan said.

"Listen to me," I snapped. "I've got a good idea for you. I'm going to give a painting lesson at my great-aunt's retirement home. Maybe you could come too and do a funny act with Mr. Badboy. I bet they'd love it."

"Cool!" Ethan replied. "Yeah. Thanks. Maybe I'll practice some new jokes with him."

"Good. Your jokes are funny, but you need some that aren't so nasty," I said.

I heard a rustling sound from the bed. Over Ethan's shoulder, I saw the dummy raise its head again. It opened its mouth and let out a long burp.

I laughed. "That's pretty good, Ethan," I said. "Come on. For real. How do you do that?"

"I'm telling the truth," Ethan said in a whisper. "I didn't do it." He grabbed my arm. "Please — believe me, Britney. Sometimes it's like . . . he comes to life or something."

I pulled my arm away. "Yeah, right. And monkeys can fly to the moon!"

But then I saw that the kid was trembling.

On the other side of the bedroom, Mr. Badboy laughed again, a high donkey bray.

I almost fell for it. But then I remembered all the dumb tricks Ethan played on me the last time he visited. He was a total trickster. He just *loved* making me look dumb.

"No way I believe you," I said. "So stop it. Give me a break. I'm trying hard to be your friend, Ethan. I want to make you feel at home here."

"*Big WHOOP!*" the dummy chimed in from the bed.

I grabbed Ethan by the shoulders. "Tell me the truth," I said. "How are you doing that?"

He lowered his head. His shoulders shook. I thought he might have tears in his eyes.

"I *am* telling the truth," he whispered. "This time, you . . . you've got to believe me, Britney."

Before I could answer, I saw the dummy raise its head. The mouth worked up and down. I could hear the click of the wooden lips.

And then the dummy screamed: "I'M ALIVE! Don't you GET it, Britney? I'M ALIVE!"

Ethan grabbed my arm and held on tight. "Help me — please!" he cried. "I . . . I don't know what to do!"

I laughed.

I remembered Ethan pretending to break his leg during his last visit. I totally panicked and called 911. After that, he made fun of me for days.

No way I was falling for this cheap joke.

"Nice try," I said. "Good acting job, Ethan. But do you really think I'm a total sucker?"

He didn't answer. Instead, he stamped down as hard as he could on my foot.

I let out a cry and hopped backward till I hit the wall.

"You jerk! That's not funny!" I screamed. "And that stupid dummy doesn't scare me."

I waited for Mr. Badboy to laugh again or say something rude. But he didn't move. He was just a dumb puppet.

I turned away from my bratty cousin. I still had some things to carry down to my new bedroom.

I gazed at my framed Skullboy poster. It

showed them rocking onstage at Radio City Music Hall in New York. And it was autographed by every member of the band.

Buzzy is my favorite band member. And he looks *awesome* in this poster with his shirt off and both fists pumping the air and all his tattoos showing.

I grabbed the edges of the frame and carefully started to lift it off the wall.

"Uh . . . Britney," Ethan said. "I think you'd better leave that poster up here in my room."

"Excuse me?" I said. "You're kidding, right?"

"Skullboy is Mr. Badboy's favorite band," Ethan said.

"Sorry. He loses," I said. "It's my favorite band, too. And I'm hanging this in my room."

Ethan tried to pull my hand off the poster frame. "Please, Britney," he said in a tiny voice.

"What is your *problem*?" I snapped.

"I . . . I want to keep Mr. Badboy happy," Ethan replied. "If I do something he doesn't like, he . . . he might hurt me."

Ethan had this terrified look on his face. He really was a good actor.

"Tough cheese," I said. "Tell you what. Sit Mr. Badboy down at the laptop. Let him go online and order his own poster."

That time I made Ethan laugh.

"Come on, you two," Mom called from downstairs. "Dinner is on the table."

"One minute!" I shouted.

I lifted the poster off the wall and carried it down to my new room. I didn't have much wall space, but the poster fit on the wall above my desk.

I carefully nailed in a picture hook and hung it next to my favorite picture — an oil painting I did of Phoebe, our old dog who died last year.

I missed Phoebe. The painting made me sad. But it was definitely my best painting — a nice way to remember her.

I made sure the Skullboy poster hung straight. Then I hurried down to dinner.

Mom had dropped a plastic jug of apple cider. She was on her knees on the kitchen floor, mopping up the spill. "I can't believe I dropped that," she muttered.

I grabbed some paper towels and helped her dry the floor. She handed me the half-empty cider jug. "*You'd* better carry it to the table," she said. "I'd drop my head if it wasn't glued on."

"I don't believe it!" I said. "We're eating in the dining room? We *never* eat in the dining room unless company is coming."

"I thought we'd make it a special celebration, because of Ethan," Mom said.

Dad was already at the table, spreading his napkin over his lap.

Dad looks like he comes from another family. He's very tall and skinny as a scarecrow. And he has short, white-blond hair and furry, white-blond eyebrows that move up and down over his blue eyes like caterpillars.

Mom calls him her Blond Freak. Dad thinks that's hilarious.

In front of him sat Mom's famous roast chicken on a blue platter, waiting to be carved. And next to it a big bowl of mashed potatoes and bowls of applesauce and string beans. A feast.

"How are you and your cousin getting along?" Dad asked.

"Peachy," I said.

Before I could say more, Ethan stepped into the room with Mr. Badboy slung over his shoulder.

Mom pointed to the chair at the end of the table. "Why don't you sit there, Ethan? Next to me," she said. She smiled at him. "Let's all sit down and get to know one another."

Ethan hesitated. He looked quickly around the table. "But you didn't set a place for Mr. Badboy," he said.

Mom and Dad exchanged glances. Dad shrugged.

"We can set a place for him across from you," Mom told Ethan. "Next to Britney."

She pulled out a place mat and napkin and set them on the table. Then she hurried into the kitchen to get silverware.

Ethan placed the dummy in its chair, then walked around the table and sat down.

Dad chuckled. "Do we have to serve him dinner?"

Suddenly, Mr. Badboy's eyes popped open wide. And he rasped, *"I'd rather eat roadkill."*

I burst out laughing.

Let's face it. Ethan really cracks me up.

Dad glared at me. "Don't laugh at that, Brit. Your mom worked hard on this dinner."

"Huh? *Me?*" I cried. "I didn't say it. *He* did!" I gave the dummy a shove.

Then I took a long sip of milk.

"Shouldn't she *pluck* the chicken before she cooks it?" Mr. Badboy cried.

I started to laugh — and choked. Milk came spurting out of my nose.

That made Ethan and me both laugh even harder.

I couldn't stop choking and laughing.

"Enough, Brit!" Dad shouted. "It's not funny."

Mom entered the room and sat down. "What's not funny?" she asked.

"Britney decided to act like a clown tonight," Dad said, frowning.

"Why are you picking on *me*?" I cried. "It's not my fault. Ethan —"

"Help yourself to some mashed potatoes," Mom said, pushing the bowl to me. She turned to Ethan. "Are you excited to have a big new room of your own?"

Before Ethan could answer, Mr. Badboy chimed in: "I'm so excited, I just peed my pants!"

I couldn't help it. I burst out laughing. The mashed potato spoon flew from my hand. A big gob of potatoes sailed across the table and smacked the front of Dad's shirt.

I watched the potatoes slide into Dad's shirt pocket. And that made me laugh so hard, I couldn't catch my breath.

"Britney, maybe you'd better leave the table and calm down," Mom said.

Dad glared at me angrily. "You're really asking for trouble," he said.

"Me? Why *me*?" I managed to choke out. "It's not *my* fault!"

"Just settle down and eat your dinner," Mom said.

"It all looks delicious," Dad said.

Once again, Mr. Badboy's mouth worked up and down. And he rasped, "I *throw up* better food than this!"

10

At school the next morning, I found Molly at a table in the back of the art room, working on her new project. Molly is even more intense about painting than I am. She has some cool ideas.

She dreams up scenes on imaginary planets and paints them. Then she downloads photos of movie and music stars off the Internet. And she prints them out and adds them to her paintings.

They're hard to describe. But Mr. Vella, our art teacher, was really excited about them. He said Molly should do at least a dozen, and maybe he could get her a show in a gallery somewhere.

I keep trying to get her to paint one with Buzzy from Skullboy. But she says she *hates* Buzzy's looks. She says she hates everything about him.

Wow.

So far, it hasn't ruined our friendship. I'm sure one of these days I can convince her she's totally wrong.

I pulled out the chair across from her and sat down. "Hey, Molly," I said. "I like the purple-and-green sky. Way cool."

She looked up from her painting. "Brit, how come you were so late this morning?"

"Ethan, of course," I said. I picked up a clean paintbrush and pretended to stab myself with the handle. "*AAAAAACK.*"

"He's a cutie-pie," Molly said sarcastically, adding brushstrokes to a clump of purple trees.

"Mom made pancakes for breakfast," I said. "You know. Ethan's first day of school. Everything has to be special for Ethan. And you know what that creep did?"

I slammed the paintbrush down on the table. "He made me laugh, and I squirted maple syrup in my hair and on my T-shirt. I had to go shampoo my hair and change. Now I'm in major trouble with Mrs. Hagerty for being late. I could *kill* that brat!"

"So things are going well!" Molly joked.

"Not funny," I muttered.

"How come he's going to school here?" Molly asked, concentrating on her trees.

"Because no one knows how long he'll be living with us. Dad dropped him off at the elementary school this morning. I have to wait around till three-thirty to pick him up."

Molly snickered. "Did he bring that ugly dummy to school with him?"

"No," I said. "He told us Mr. Badboy likes to sleep late."

"He's totally mental," Molly said. "Does he believe it's alive or something?"

"The little clown is trying to make ME believe it's alive," I said. "What a joke."

Molly narrowed her eyes at me. "So you don't believe it?"

"Huh? Believe Mr. Badboy is alive?" I said. "Of *course* not."

That night, I had dinner at Molly's house. Her dad was off on another long trip. Margie, the housekeeper who always stays with Molly when her dad is away, ordered us a pepperoni pizza and a couple of salads, and we had ice-cream pops for dessert.

Was I happy? Well, yes. Pepperoni is my favorite. But mainly, I didn't have to sit across the table from Ethan.

After dinner, Molly and I were in front of her laptop, checking out the latest gossip on Face Place, our school's message board. Molly's bedroom is almost as small as my new room. She's covered one whole wall from floor to ceiling with her paintings, and it looks really awesome.

"Guess who wants to bring his dummy to school tomorrow?" I asked.

Molly shook her head. "Doesn't he care that kids will think he's a geek?"

I shrugged. "I don't get it. Guess he just wants attention."

"My dad said he's seen Ethan's dummy before," Molly said. "He just can't remember where."

"Let's not talk about it," I muttered. I glanced at the clock. Almost eight-thirty. "I'd better go home and write that essay," I said. "I'm already on Mrs. Hagerty's bad list."

"Whoa. Check this out," Molly said, eyes bulging at the laptop screen. "Cindy Siegel's photos from her party last week. Oh, wow. I can't believe she put these online. If her parents ever saw them . . ."

I ended up spending another hour at Molly's. Then I hurried home to write the essay. It was due tomorrow, and I knew I couldn't afford to mess up.

Mom and Dad were in the den, watching a movie on TV. The house smelled of popcorn. They have popcorn almost every night. They say it's low calorie, but they eat huge bowls of it!

I started up the stairs to the attic — then remembered it wasn't my room anymore. So I turned around, made my way down the hall, and stepped into the little sewing room.

I flashed on the ceiling light — and gasped. "Oh, nooo . . ."

My poster.

My Skullboy poster.

The glass frame was cracked and shattered.

I saw jagged shards of glass on the floor.

I stood frozen in the doorway, unable to take another step into the room. My eyes stared at the shattered glass.

And then I saw the long rip down the middle of the poster. It had been torn in half. And Buzzy's face . . . it was gone. Torn off the poster.

My heart pounded in my chest. I suddenly felt cold all over, as if the room had turned to ice.

I blinked several times, trying to force the sight away.

And then my eyes stopped on the painting of Phoebe. I let out another gasp when I saw the red mustache smeared on the dog's snout. And splashes of red paint covering the dog's eyes.

"Owwww!" I was squeezing my fists so tight, my fingernails were digging into my palms.

I took a deep breath. Then another. But I couldn't calm down.

"This is the last straw, Ethan," I muttered through gritted teeth. "This isn't funny. This is mean and vicious."

I spun around and started toward the attic stairs.

What did I plan to do? I don't know. I couldn't think straight. The blotchy red mustache stayed in front of my eyes. I was actually *seeing red*!

I wanted to tear Ethan in half — just the way he tore my poster.

I stomped up the stairs. My hands were still balled into tight fists.

"Too far," I muttered. "This time, you went too far."

I burst into the room, dark except for the pale, low light from a tiny night-light down on the floor. I nearly tripped over the pile of dirty clothes Ethan had dropped in the middle of the carpet.

Kicking a pair of jeans out of my way, I stormed up to Ethan's bed. "Ethan —?"

It took a while for my eyes to focus in the dim gray light. And then I saw the dummy, stretched out on the bed, his head resting on the pillow.

"Ethan —?"

Not there. Ethan was not in the bed.

Huh?

I heard the shower going downstairs in the bathroom. Ethan must be in the shower, I realized.

I stood frozen for a moment, clenching and unclenching my fists.

And then I jumped back as the dummy moved.

The head jerked. Mr. Badboy sat up quickly. The blue eyes blinked open with a wooden click.

The ugly dummy turned its stare on me.

And uttered in a hoarse whisper: *"I DON'T LIKE YOU, BRITNEY!"*

11

My breath caught in my throat. I staggered back till I hit the wall.

The dummy stared at me with that ugly grin. Then he slowly lowered himself back onto his pillow.

This can't be happening! I told myself.

But it is. Something terrifying is going on here.

Ethan is downstairs. The dummy sat up on its own.

And SPOKE!

And it HATES me!

My legs trembled as I forced myself away from the wall. I kept my gaze on Mr. Badboy. His eyes stayed wide open, staring up at the ceiling. But he didn't move again.

I lurched toward the door. Stumbled over the jeans on the floor. Staggered to the attic stairs, breathing hard.

"I DON'T LIKE YOU, BRITNEY!"

The dummy's hoarse rasp repeated in my ears.

"You're not alive!" I cried, taking the stairs two at a time. "You can't be alive!"

I couldn't keep this to myself. I was too frightened. I had to tell Mom and Dad.

I burst into the den. The room was dark except for the darting glare from the screen. They always turn out the lights when they watch a movie.

They were on the couch, sitting close together, bowls of popcorn on their laps. Mom jumped as I came lurching in. She made a grab for the popcorn bowl, but it toppled to the floor. Popcorn spilled everywhere.

"Britney, you startled me!" she cried. "Look what you made me do!"

Dad paused the movie. He narrowed his eyes at me. "What on earth is your problem?"

"I — I —" I stammered. "Something —" I gasped for breath.

Dad pulled me to the couch. I dropped down next to Mom. "You're trembling," Mom said. "Are you sick? Do you have a fever?"

"It's the . . . dummy," I finally choked out. "Ethan's dummy."

They both stared at me.

"It's crazy," I said. "I know it. But I'm telling the truth. It's alive. It's really alive!"

Mom wrapped her arm around my shoulders. "Take a deep breath, Brit," she said softly. "You're not making any sense."

"Start at the beginning," Dad said. "We don't understand what you're saying. What about Ethan's dummy?"

I took a deep breath and let it out. "My painting of Phoebe. It . . . it's *ruined*! And my Skullboy poster was ripped in half. I knew Ethan did it. So I ran up to his room."

"Your Skullboy poster?" Mom interrupted. "Are you sure the frame didn't just fall off the wall?"

"I'm sure," I said. "I ran up to Ethan's room. And he wasn't there. He was in the shower. But . . . the dummy. It . . . it SAT UP!"

I saw Mom and Dad exchange a glance. Mom pressed her hand on my forehead.

"I don't have a fever!" I screamed, and I shoved her hand away. "Listen to me. The dummy sat up on its own. And it talked. It said, 'I don't like you, Britney.' I'm not making this up. That's what it said to me."

"You fell asleep," Dad said, rubbing his chin. "You had a nightmare. Remember? You used to sleepwalk?"

"Dad, that was when I was *three*!" I cried. "I wasn't asleep! I just got home from Molly's. I was wide-awake."

I jumped to my feet, my whole body trembling. "Are you going to believe me or not?"

Mom patted the couch cushion. "Sit down, Brit."

I shook my head and crossed my arms in front of me.

47

"How can we believe you?" Dad said. "It's crazy."

"The dummy didn't talk on its own," Mom said. "Ethan was playing a trick on you. I'll bet he was under the bed. Or hiding in the closet."

"I think you've been spending too much time at the Molloys'," Dad said. "Wild Man Molloy and his weirdo dolls. They've put strange ideas in your head, Brit." He shrugged. "Maybe you shouldn't see so much of Molly."

"Huh?" I let out an angry cry. "Now I'm going to lose my *best friend* because of that evil little creep Ethan?"

"Don't call him an evil little creep," Mom snapped. "He's your cousin. He's family. And he needs our help."

"We need you to be the grown-up," Dad said. "Making up crazy stories about dummies coming to life isn't going to help anyone."

"Dad, I'm not making this up," I said in a trembling voice. My hands were balled into tight fists again. I could feel myself totally losing it.

I bit my lips till they hurt. *No way* I was going to start sobbing now.

"I know it sounds crazy," I said. "But the dummy is alive. And it's *evil*!"

They both stared at me. As if I were crazy.

I spun around and ran from the den. I hurtled into my room and slammed the door.

I threw myself onto the bed. But I didn't cry. I was too angry to cry.

My own parents refused to listen to me. Refused to *believe* me. My own parents treated me as if I were a nut.

I turned and gazed at my torn poster, my dog portrait with the ugly red splotches smeared over it.

There they were, my two favorite things, ruined. Destroyed. I didn't make it up. The proof was there on the wall.

I tiptoed to the door and listened. Did my parents just shrug off my story and go back to their movie?

No. It was quiet down there. They were probably cleaning up the spilled popcorn and discussing what to do with their problem daughter.

I picked up my cell to call Molly. But I realized it was too late to call.

I'll never get to sleep, I thought. *How can I sleep knowing there's something evil in my house?*

I changed into my nightshirt, climbed into bed, and pulled the blankets over my head. But I could still see the torn poster . . . the red paint on my painting . . . the dummy . . . the evil dummy raising his head and spouting those ugly words: *"I don't like you, Britney."*

Somehow, I fell into a deep, dreamless sleep.

The next morning, I pulled on jeans and a

sweater and got myself ready for school. I felt weary, as if I hadn't slept at all. Every time I glanced at the poster and painting, my stomach tightened in cold dread.

I looked out my window. It was a gray morning. Dark clouds hung low in the sky. The darkness matched my mood.

I left my room and headed for the stairs. I could smell coffee from the kitchen. And bacon frying.

I heard footsteps behind me and glimpsed Ethan coming down the attic stairs, holding Mr. Badboy in front of him.

I pretended I didn't see him and started down the steps.

I was almost halfway down when I heard Ethan's shout close behind me: "Britney — *watch out!*"

"Hey —!"

I uttered a cry as I felt hard wooden hands shove my back.

Stumbling, I grabbed for the banister.

Missed.

And started to fall headfirst down the stairs.

12

"Ohhh —!"

I tucked my head under my arms and bumped hard all the way down.

"Ow. Ow. Ow." I landed on my back, still shielding my head, gasping for breath. Too stunned to move.

I lay there, waiting for the pain to fade. I stared up at Ethan and Mr. Badboy, still on the stairs.

Ethan's face had gone pale. His eyes were wide with shock. "Britney — are you all right?" he cried in a tiny, frightened voice.

He came running down to me. The dummy bounced in his arms.

"What's going on?" Mom called from the kitchen.

"Britney fell!" Ethan shouted.

I didn't fall, I thought. *The dummy pushed me!*

I rubbed my elbow. It throbbed with pain. But the rest of me seemed okay.

51

Ethan grabbed my hand and tried to pull me up.

Mom came running, a metal spatula in one hand. "Oh, no! Britney? Did you fall down the stairs?"

"Just a few of them," I said. "No big deal, Mom."

Why tell the truth? Would she believe me if I said the dummy pushed me?

Yeah. For sure. She'd blame my wild imagination. Or she'd say I watch too many horror movies.

I climbed to my feet, rubbing my sore elbow. "I'm okay. Really."

"My bacon's burning," Mom said. "Come have your breakfast." She turned and hurried back to the stove.

I glared at Ethan. "You and I have to talk," I said.

He turned his head away. He looked very frightened. Then he looked back and said, "Listen, Brit, I —"

But before he could say any more, the dummy lowered his head to my ear — and whispered in his cold, hoarse voice: *"Don't ever snitch on me again!"*

13

The rest of the day was a blur. I couldn't get that dummy's whispered words out of my mind. I was desperate to tell Molly about it. But she was away all day on some kind of science field trip.

I phoned her after school, but she couldn't talk. She was going to visit some cousins in the next town over.

She didn't call me back until late that night. I was pulling on my nightshirt and getting ready for bed when my cell phone rang. She started talking before I even answered.

"Molly? What's wrong?" I asked. She sounded totally freaked.

"Britney, hurry," she said. "You've got to help me. We have to bury it."

Huh?

"Molly, what are you talking about?" I whispered. I'm not allowed to talk on the phone so late at night.

"The doll," Molly said breathlessly. "That awful

thing with the shrunken head. I can't leave it in the house. Please — come over. I need your help."

"But it's after eleven," I whispered. "If I get caught —"

"Britney, this is life or death," Molly said. "I'm not joking. I *need* you!"

"I'll get dressed," I said. "I'll sneak out the back door. Give me two minutes."

Two minutes later, I was running through backyards and across the street to Molly's house. The grass was slippery and wet due to the weather. I lowered my head against the strong gusts of wind.

Molly's house was dark except for a light in the attic window. But she stood waiting for me at the back door. She grabbed my arm and pulled me into the kitchen.

She had already pulled on a yellow rain slicker and had the hood lowered over her head. "We have to hurry," she whispered.

"Molly, I — I don't understand," I said. "Tell me. What's up with that doll?"

She brushed back the rain hood. I could see the fear in her eyes. "The Mind Stealer. My dad — he was wrong. We have to bury it. In a graveyard."

I narrowed my eyes at her. "You're not joking? Where's your dad?"

"On an island somewhere," she said. "Near Australia, I think. I tried to call him. I don't think his cell is working."

"But . . . why do we have to bury that doll? That's just crazy — isn't it?"

"A man called me," Molly said. "A few minutes ago. From Mumba. He said my dad asked him for information about the Mind Stealer doll. And . . . and . . ."

"Molly, what did he say?" I asked.

"He said he did research for my dad. He talked to people in Mumba. The doll's powers are deadly strong. It shouldn't be kept in the house. My dad didn't know. It has to be buried in . . . a graveyard."

I stared at her. "He was serious?"

"Very serious," Molly said. "He said to get the doll out of the house tonight. He said maybe it's all just an old legend. But we shouldn't take chances. It's too dangerous."

She grabbed my hand. "You've got to help me, Brit. I'm really scared. I knew that doll was trouble. My dad — he — sometimes he just doesn't take things seriously."

"What about Margie?" I asked. "Your housekeeper. Can she help us?"

"She has the flu," Molly replied. "I can't ask her to come out."

Molly stared at the glass case in fear. "I'll carry the doll case." She shivered. "There's a shovel in the garage. You can carry that."

And that's how Molly and I ended up in the little graveyard three blocks away from our houses.

Nearly midnight. The neighborhood dark. No cars in the street. No moon in the cloud-covered sky. Cold raindrops pattering down on us.

There we were, taking turns shoveling up the hard dirt.

Inside the glass case, the evil doll stared up at us with its empty eye sockets in its shriveled green head. The wind howled. The old gravestones creaked and groaned.

Could we get the evil doll buried before it did something *horrible* to us?

Could it get any scarier?

Yes.

The hole was at least two feet deep. Almost deep enough. I dug the shovel blade into the dirt.

And that's when the old gravestone across from me tilted forward. I saw crumbling dirt at the bottom of the stone.

And then I saw the pale hand reach out from behind it.

Too late. I saw it too late to escape its grip.

It grabbed me around the ankle. Wrapped its cold fingers over my skin.

And I let out a shrill scream.

"Ethan —!" I gasped. "What are you *doing* here?"

"Made you scream!" he said. He let go of my ankle. Then he jumped out from behind the tombstone and did a little dance, laughing like a hyena.

Molly gave him a hard shove, and he fell back against an old granite slab. "You brat!" she snapped. "You followed us here?"

He grinned. "You're burying that stupid doll? You're both totally mental."

The rain came down harder, drumming the ground. I pretended to strangle Ethan. "I'd like to bury *you*!" I said.

"I know what happens at midnight," Ethan said. "You both turn into pumpkins!"

"This isn't a joke," Molly said angrily. "Get away, Ethan." She shoved him again. "Unless you want to help us. We have to bury this thing. It really *does* steal minds."

Ethan giggled. "You're both out of your minds already!"

A flash of lightning made the ugly Mind Stealer doll appear to move. I felt a chill roll down my back.

I dug the shovel deep into the hole and scooped out another clump of dirt. "I . . . I think it's deep enough," I said.

Ethan watched as Molly and I carefully . . . carefully . . . lifted the glass case. The disgusting little head rolled to one side. The doll's wooden arms bounced against the glass.

Into the hole. We lowered it slowly. The glass case felt slippery and wet from the rain. But we set it down in the hole. Then we both frantically shoveled and scooped dirt over it.

Buried it.

Buried it out of sight. Where its evil powers could do no damage.

And then the three of us ran for home, battered by the wind and rain.

Molly had a smile on her face now. At least she could feel safe again in her own house.

But what about me? No way I could feel safe. Not with a living dummy turning my life into a horror show. . . .

14

"Mom, please don't make me take Ethan," I begged.

Mom bit her bottom lip. "Britney, you have no choice," she said. "You promised him, remember? You have to take him."

She straightened her hair in the front hall mirror and picked up the car keys. It was nearly four the next afternoon. She was ready to drive us to perform at Sunset House, my great-aunt's retirement home.

"Britney, do you have all your art supplies packed up? Put them in the trunk," she said.

She started to the door, but I grabbed her arm. "Mom, you're not listening to me," I said. "If we take Ethan, something terrible is going to happen."

"Stop it — right now," she said. "Go call your cousin. He's upstairs practicing his comedy act."

My throat felt tight and dry. "I know you don't believe me," I said, "but I'm not making this up.

Mr. Badboy is *alive*, Mom. He's alive — and he's evil!"

Mom slammed the car keys down on the hallway shelf. She glared at me angrily. "Enough," she said. "Enough, enough, enough. You're acting like a total baby, Britney."

"But, Mom. I can prove it," I said.

She raised a hand. "Enough. Enough. Not another word. I mean it. Not another word about that dummy."

My breath caught in my throat. I felt so hurt and angry. Mom always believed me before Ethan came to live with us. She always trusted me. She always talked about how grown-up I was. And now . . .

She pointed to the stairs. "Go get Ethan. Great-aunt Ruth is waiting."

I let out a long sigh and started up the stairs. I knew if I brought Ethan and Mr. Badboy with me, something terrible would happen.

But what could I do?

A short while later, Mom pulled the car up the long driveway to Sunset House. We passed by tall hedges and a rolling lawn with beds of red and yellow flowers. People sat in chairs around a bubbling fountain, talking and reading.

The house was a tall brick building. The afternoon sunlight reflected off the many windows, making the whole house appear to glow.

I pulled my art supplies from the trunk and waved to Mom as she drove away. Great-aunt Ruth was waiting for Ethan and me in the front hall.

She is almost eighty-five, but she looks a lot younger. She has short, straight black hair, and she wears a lot of makeup and bright red lipstick. Today she wore faded jeans with embroidery on the pockets and a pale blue shirt that tied at the waist. After giving Ethan and me bone-crushing hugs, she began chattering a mile a minute, asking about everyone in the family.

A short, plump gray-haired woman wearing a gray pants suit stepped up with a smile. "Britney, this is so nice of you," she said.

"Hi, Mrs. Berman," I said. She's the director of the house. "This is my cousin Ethan. He's going to perform with his dummy."

"How excellent," she said. "Come this way. Your audience is waiting for you in the rec room."

We followed her down the hall and into the room. Folding chairs had been set up in three rows. About twenty people turned when we came in. Most of them were white-haired. Two were in wheelchairs, and I saw a lot of canes and walkers.

I put down my paint case and started to set up my easel. Ethan took a seat in a corner and plopped Mr. Badboy on his lap.

"This is Ruth's niece, Britney Crosby," Mrs. Berman announced. "She is going to give you all a painting lesson. And then Britney's cousin Evan is going to put on a puppet show."

"It's *Ethan*!" Mr. Badboy shouted.

People began to murmur. A few people laughed.

I opened my paint jars and turned to the audience. "I know a lot of you like to draw and paint," I said. "So I thought —"

"Louder, please!" a woman in the front row shouted.

"So I thought today I'd —"

"She's deaf!" another woman called out. "She won't hear you no matter how loud you shout."

A lot of people laughed. Great-aunt Ruth turned in her seat and shushed everyone.

I took a deep breath and continued. "Since we're in Sunset House, I thought I'd show you how to paint a beautiful sunset with just two colors — red and yellow."

I picked up the brush and began to mix colors.

"Maybe she could paint my room!" a man in the back row said to the woman next to him.

"Maybe she could paint my *nails*!" the woman said.

They were both shouting. They must have been nearly deaf. I could feel my legs start to shake. Mom had warned me it would be a tough audience.

I turned and saw Great-aunt Ruth smiling at

me. I decided to keep my eyes on her for the rest of the demonstration.

"What is she painting?"

"I don't get this modern art!"

"Look. She dripped on the floor."

I should have worn earplugs! But I hummed to myself to drown them out. And I kept working my brush on the canvas. The sunset painting turned out really well, maybe the best sunset I'd ever done.

And when I stepped away from it, everyone cheered and clapped, even the woman who wanted me to paint her nails. Great-aunt Ruth blew me a kiss. I could tell how proud she was.

I felt really happy. But then I remembered what was coming next, and my stomach tightened in dread.

"Here's Ethan," I announced to everyone, "with his good friend Mr. Badboy." As Ethan passed me, I whispered, "Don't mess up."

"I'll try," he whispered back.

Why did he look so frightened?

15

Ethan pulled his folding chair to the front of the room. He sat down and bounced the dummy on his lap.

"Which one is Ethan?" a woman whispered loudly. A few people laughed.

Ethan cleared his throat and turned to the grinning dummy. "You're going to be a good boy today, aren't you, Mr. Badboy?"

Mr. Badboy shook his head no. "I'm a BAAAAAAD boy! Know how I can tell when someone is *old*?" he asked Ethan.

"How?"

"By the *smell*!" Mr. Badboy tossed back his head and cackled.

"That's not funny," Ethan scolded him.

"Yeah," Mr. Badboy shot back. "That joke STINKS! And so do they!"

A few people gasped. The room grew very quiet.

Mr. Badboy's jaws clicked up and down. "Ethan,

do you know the difference between an old person and roadkill?"

"No," Ethan said.

"Neither do I!" Mr. Badboy cried, and laughed his high-pitched laugh again.

"That is not allowed!" Mrs. Berman shouted from the back of the room. "Ethan, your jokes are insulting people."

"Your FACE is insulting ME!" Mr. Badboy exclaimed. "I've seen PIMPLES that were prettier than you!"

I shut my eyes. I just wanted to disappear. This couldn't be happening!

"I'm a BAAAAAAD boy!" Mr. Badboy shouted.

He turned his head to a woman with curly white hair and bright red lips. "Is that a new skirt?" the dummy asked her. "Or are you wearing your intestines on the *outside*?"

Mrs. Berman stormed toward the front of the room, swinging tight fists at her sides. Her face was as red as my sunset painting. "Ethan, I have to ask you to stop," she said.

Ethan jumped up. "I'm really sorry," he said. "Sometimes Mr. Badboy acts up. But I know he'll be good now."

Mrs. Berman glared at him. "Your jokes are not acceptable!"

"I promise he'll behave," Ethan said. He shot me a nervous glance. Then he turned back to the audience. "I need a volunteer. Could you come up and talk to Mr. Badboy, ma'am? I promise he'll be good. Please — come up here."

I realized I was holding my breath. What did Ethan plan to do?

Or more important — what did *Mr. Badboy* plan to do?

Ethan kept pleading with her. So finally, a gray-haired woman in a flowery brown-and-yellow housedress stood up and slowly walked up beside the grinning dummy.

She shook Mr. Badboy's hand. "Are you going to be a *good* boy?" she asked, grinning at Ethan.

Mr. Badboy's eyes blinked up and down. "I like your dress," he said. "Interesting colors. Or did you spit up your breakfast this morning?"

I gasped. Now I knew for sure. I had no doubts at all. The dummy was alive — and out of control.

The woman laughed. "You're naughty," she said. "Someone should *spank* you!"

"I'd like to spank you, too," Mr. Badboy replied. "But with that face, I can't tell *which end* to spank!"

I turned and saw Mrs. Berman shaking her head and frowning.

"Which color do you like in Britney's painting?" Mr. Badboy asked the woman. "The red or the yellow?"

She studied my painting for a moment. "The red, I guess."

And then . . . it all happened so quickly, it was a total blur.

I saw the jar of red paint swing up into the air. Was it in Mr. Badboy's hand? Or did Ethan hold the jar?

I couldn't see. But I saw the jar swing high — and I saw the red paint come splashing out.

It made a loud *SPLAAATTTT* as it burst over the woman's face. It ran down her cheeks, down her skirt, and puddled on her shoes.

Her mouth dropped open in shock. She staggered back, wiping paint from her eyes. But Mr. Badboy wasn't finished.

Now the yellow paint jar was in the air. And a tidal wave of thick yellow paint splashed over the woman's hair.

"I'm a BAAAAAAD boy!" Mr. Badboy shouted.

Mrs. Berman leaped forward and tried to pull the dummy from Ethan's arms. And I rushed to the front of the room, my brain spinning. I knew I had to do something to help.

But I tripped over my easel. The whole thing collapsed under me, and I fell facedown on my painting.

"Ohhh." I groaned and tried to pull myself to my feet. Smears of red and yellow paint stuck to the front of my sweater.

67

I heard people stampeding from the room. Some were crying. Others were shouting angrily.

A disaster, I thought. *A total disaster*.

Raising my eyes, I glared at the ugly dummy. And as I stared, he tossed back his head and roared with laughter.

16

"Molly, where is your dad? I have to talk to him."

That night, I was too upset to eat dinner. I rushed up to my room and slammed the door behind me. Then I dropped onto the edge of my bed and punched Molly's number into my cell phone.

"I told you," Molly replied. "He's on some island near Australia. I haven't heard a word from him since he left."

"Well, when is he coming back?" My voice cracked. "It's a real emergency."

Molly was silent for a moment. "Brit, come over. You'll feel better if you get out of the house."

"I can't," I moaned. "I'm grounded. Probably for life. Mrs. Berman at Sunset House? She reported the whole thing to school. I don't believe it, but she blamed *me* for everything. She said I invited Ethan, so I had to know what kind of jokes he did. She said I had to know what Ethan planned to do."

"Oh, wow," Molly muttered. "Bad news. That's totally unfair."

"Tell me about it," I groaned. "Then Mrs. Berman called my mom and told her about it. I'm *so* in trouble everywhere. I'm not allowed to leave my room at night. And . . . and meanwhile, get this. Dad had hockey tickets that he couldn't return. So he took Ethan to the hockey game. It's *so* not fair!"

"Ethan is a total freak," Molly said. "I can't believe he's your cousin."

"Ethan isn't the problem," I said. "It's Mr. Badboy. He's alive, Molly. He's evil — and Ethan is too scared to do anything about it."

"But, Brit —"

"Molly, I'm *begging* you to believe me," I said. "No one else will. I'm not even allowed to mention the dummy to my mom or dad. But your dad . . . he'd believe me. He knows about this stuff — right?"

"Well . . ." Molly said, "Dad has done research on ventriloquist's dummies. I know he's collected a lot of magazine articles and papers. Come over, Brit. Sneak out and come over. We can try to find his file."

I was totally desperate. So I sneaked out the back door and ran all the way to Molly's house.

She greeted me in a pale blue T-shirt and red-and-white boxers. She had just washed her hair and had a red bath towel wrapped around her head like a turban.

We turned on as many lights in the attic as we could. But the room still gave me the creeps, with ugly stuffed creatures and strange dolls staring out at us from the glass cases.

I stopped to gaze at the empty shelf that had held the Mind Stealer doll. A shiver rolled down my back as I pictured the graveyard in the rain.

Molly pulled me into her dad's library at the far end of the attic. One wall was lined with tall gray file cabinets. We began pawing through the file drawers, bulging with articles and magazines and photos and research papers about all the weird stuff Mr. Molloy was into.

After about twenty minutes of searching, I pulled out a heavy file marked VENTRILOQUISM. "Molly — check it out!" I said. I lugged it to the desk, spread it open, and Molly and I began sifting through all the papers.

Molly wrinkled her forehead. "What exactly are we looking for?"

I sighed. "Anything that will help me prove to my parents that Mr. Badboy has to be destroyed. I — I —"

My words caught in my throat. I stared at the wrinkled and faded black-and-white photo in front of me.

"I don't *believe* it!" I gasped. "It's Ethan's dummy. Look!"

Molly lowered her face to the photo and studied it. "The same chip on its bottom lip," she murmured. "The same wicked smile."

"The same ugly grin," I said. My hand trembled as I picked up the photo and turned it over. The back was covered in tiny type. I squinted to read it.

"It says the dummy's real name is *Slappy*," I told Molly. "And — and I was right! He's totally evil!"

My heart pounded as I scanned the words. "It says Slappy was made by a magician sometime in the late 1800s," I said. "An evil sorcerer. The wood he used was cursed. He built the dummy from a stolen coffin."

Molly blinked. "Oh, wow. I wish Dad was here. . . ."

"It says the dummy turns its owners into slaves," I continued. "It's power mad. It wants to enslave everyone it meets. And — and —"

My eyes skipped to the bottom. I gasped and grabbed Molly's arm. "Listen to this, Molly! It has a bunch of weird words at the bottom of the page. It says, 'Say these six ancient words to wake him up. And to put him to sleep.'"

"You're kidding!" Molly grabbed the photo from my hands and stared at it. "This is *excellent*, Britney. What are we waiting for?"

She handed the photo back to me. Then she unwound the towel from her head and began drying her coppery hair.

"Come on — hurry, Brit. Let's do it. Let's shout the words in front of Slappy and put him back to sleep forever. You said Ethan is away at a hockey game — right?"

As we raced down the attic stairs, I raised the photo and read the ancient words silently one more time.

Were my worries over?

Would the words put Slappy to sleep?

17

I slipped into my house through the back door. I signaled to Molly to be quiet. Then we tiptoed across the kitchen to the front hall.

I heard the thud of dance music from the den and glimpsed Mom on the couch with a magazine in her lap. Mom doesn't dance, but she loves disco music, the louder the better.

So she didn't hear Molly and me as we hurried up the stairs and then made our way into the attic.

Ethan had left all the lights on in his room. The place was a mess. He had dirty clothes heaped everywhere, PlayStation game disks and manga comics scattered over the floor, an open bag of Cheez Doodles on his computer keyboard, empty soda cans and balled-up jeans on his bed.

Molly and I stepped through the mess to the far end of the room. Slappy was propped up in the brown leather armchair by the window. The dummy's hands rested on the chair arms. He stared straight ahead.

"We know your secret, Slappy," I said. My voice sounded funny — shrill and tight. My chest felt all fluttery. I tapped the dummy's wooden head. "See? I even know your real name."

I expected him to move or speak. But he just kept staring at the other wall.

Molly dropped down on the edge of Ethan's cluttered bed. I could see she was frightened, too. "Don't mess around," she said softly. "Read the words. Before he does something horrible."

I held the photo tightly in both hands to keep them from shaking. "Good-bye forever, Slappy," I said.

And then slowly I whispered the ancient words. . . .

"*'Karru marri odonna loma molonu karrano.'*"

Silence.

I could hear the blood throbbing in my ears.

And then I gasped as the dummy's hands slipped off the chair arms. And he slumped forward until his head rested in his lap.

He stayed there, limp and lifeless.

I stood waiting . . . waiting and watching. But he didn't move again.

Then I spun around and pumped both fists in the air. "We did it, Molly!" I cried happily. "We put him to sleep!"

I expected Molly to jump up and celebrate, too.

But she didn't move. She stared hard at something on the bed.

"Molly? What's your problem?" I cried. "We did it! We're okay now. We put him to sleep!"

"Uh . . . wait a sec, Brit," Molly murmured. "There's something here I think you should see."

18

Molly reached into the pocket of Ethan's crumpled jeans and pulled out a small rectangular object.

It looked like a TV clicker. She dropped it onto the bed.

"Why was this hanging out of Ethan's pocket?" Molly asked.

I picked it up and rolled it around in my hand. It had at least a dozen red buttons on the front but no words. No words anywhere on it.

I pushed the top button. Then I gasped as Slappy began to move. He raised his head and laughed.

"Weird!" Molly said. "Push it again."

I pushed the same button. Slappy raised his head and laughed again.

"What's up with this?" I cried.

I aimed the clicker at Slappy and pushed another button.

"I'M ALIVE!" the dummy screamed in its tinny rasp of a voice. "DON'T YOU GET IT, BRITNEY? I'M ALIVE!"

I pushed another button.

"Don't ever snitch on me again!" the dummy said in a whisper.

I pushed it again.

"Don't ever snitch on me again!"

My hand shook as I aimed the controller at Slappy and pushed another button.

"I don't like you, Britney."

"AAAAAGH!" I let out an angry cry and heaved the clicker to the bed. "He did it again!" I screamed. "That creep Ethan did it to me again!"

I grabbed up the jeans and threw them across the floor. I turned over the Cheez Doodles bag and emptied it on his keyboard. I knew I was totally losing it. But I couldn't control my . . . my FURY.

"He must be some kind of electronics genius," Molly said. "The dummy has a computer chip, right? Ethan recorded all those things it said. He deliberately did it all to scare you."

"It . . . it's so totally mean," I said, fighting back tears. "Ethan spilled the paint on that woman at Sunset House. And insulted those people. And . . . ripped my poster in half. And he acted so frightened, like he didn't have any control over the dummy. All an act. All a stupid act!"

I tore at both sides of my hair. *"AAAAAGGGH.* I knew Ethan was trouble," I said. "But I never dreamed he was so mean and vicious."

Molly climbed to her feet. "What are you going to do now?"

I let out a long sigh. "I . . . don't know."

"Are you going to tell him you know what he did?" Molly demanded. "Are you going to tell your parents? Or are you going to wait a while and get your revenge?"

"I . . . don't know," I repeated, my mind spinning.

A smile slowly spread across my face. "But I know one thing for sure, Molly. I'm going to get a good night's sleep tonight. No more reason to be scared. I'm *never* going to worry about that stupid dummy again."

I felt a soft tap on my shoulder.

"Huh?" I blinked.

Another tap.

I was having the nicest dream. But it vanished as my eyes opened. My brain slowly woke up.

Yawning, I glimpsed my bed-table alarm clock. It was 2:35 in the morning.

I felt another tap on my shoulder, harder this time.

Now I was fully awake. I rolled around and squinted into the darkness. "Ethan? What do you want?"

And then I opened my mouth in a frightened cry. "Slappy —!"

The dummy lowered his grinning face. The big blue eyes locked on mine. His wooden hand shot out — and grabbed my wrist.

"Thanks," he whispered in my ear. "Thanks for waking me up, SLAVE!"

19

The wooden fingers tightened around my wrist. Tighter . . . until I wanted to scream. Pain shot up my arm.

"Let go of me!" I cried.

The dummy lowered his face over me until our noses nearly touched. "Thank you, slave," he rasped. "You called out the words to wake me up."

"No —!" I gasped. "I didn't mean to. I —"

He snickered an ugly laugh from deep in his throat. "You're my slave now, Britney. You'll do whatever I say."

"Why should I?" I choked out, struggling to pull my wrist free. "My mom and dad will —"

"Go ahead. Tell your parents," he said. He snickered again. "Go ahead. I'd like that. Know what they'll think? They'll think you've gone crazy. They won't believe a word. They'll take you to a doctor."

He released my wrist. His painted grin appeared to grow wider. "Are you ready for your first task?"

"N-no," I stammered. "Go away. You can't force me to do anything."

He uttered a low growl and straightened up. Then he raised both fists in front of me. "I can hurt you, Britney," he snarled. "I'm not playing games. Get up and get dressed."

"Why? Wh-what do you want?" I stammered.

"You're going to take a short trip," Slappy said. "Back to that graveyard. I heard that little freak Ethan talking about the Mind Stealer you buried. I WANT it! I NEED it!"

He gave me a hard shove with both wooden hands. "Go get it, Britney. Dig it up and bring it to me."

I rolled out of bed and landed on my feet. My heart thudded in my chest. But I suddenly felt more angry than afraid.

No way I was going to take orders from a wooden dummy!

"Out of my face!" I shouted. I lowered my shoulder and grabbed Slappy around the waist. My plan was to lift him off the floor and heave him out of my room.

"Ooooh!" I uttered a groan as I strained to pull him up.

He wouldn't budge.

"Nice try, Brit," he said. "Here. Hit me in the

stomach. Hit me as hard as you can." He stuck out his skinny stomach and giggled.

I took a step back. I tried to remember the six ancient words to put him to sleep forever.

Think, Britney. Think, I told myself.

It was useless. I couldn't remember them.

Maybe this was more evil than I could handle, but I wasn't going back to that graveyard. I wasn't going to be his slave. No way.

I crossed my arms in front of me. "I'm . . . not . . . going . . . back . . . to . . . that . . . graveyard," I said slowly, through gritted teeth.

He froze there and stared at me for the longest time. Long enough for chill after chill to shiver my body.

"No problem," he whispered finally. "Fine with me, Brit. *I'll* go get it. But when I have that doll, *your* mind will be the first to be sucked dry. Then you'll be a *perfect* slave, won't you, my dear!"

20

He spun away from me and started walking out of my room. He walked stiffly, not bending his knees, his shoulders teetering from side to side — like a zombie in a horror movie.

Frozen in terror, I couldn't move.

Clump. Clump. Clump.

I listened to him thump down the stairs. A few seconds later, I heard the front door close behind him.

He's really doing it. He's going to the grave-yard to get the doll, I realized.

I had to stop him. I bolted into the hall — then stopped. I realized I was in my nightshirt.

I lurched back into my room, grabbed jeans and a sweatshirt, pulled on my sneakers, and hurried out of the house.

It was a cool, clear night. Thin snakes of black cloud curled over a full moon. My shoes squished over the slippery grass as I ran to the street.

It must have rained earlier. Puddles of silver moonlight glowed in the street.

I saw Slappy clumping through the puddles. He swung his arms as he stormed up the low hill that led to the graveyard. He kept his back straight and tall, his head straight forward as he staggered up the middle of the road.

The cool night air helped wake me up. I started to trot. I didn't want to catch up with him. But I didn't want to lose sight of him, either.

My heart thumped loudly. In the late-night silence, nothing moved. No wind. No cars or voices. The houses all dark. As if Slappy and I were the only two creatures on earth.

Stepping over the silvery puddles, I followed Slappy to the little graveyard. I watched from the other side of the picket fence as he made his way quickly through the rows of crooked gravestones.

He stopped at the spot where we buried the Mind Stealer doll. And dropped to his knees.

My breath caught in my throat. I watched him start to scoop up dirt. His wooden hands made good shovels. The dirt flew up in front of him.

I knew I should leap over the fence. Drop him. Smother him. Crush him. Do *anything* to keep him from pulling up that dangerous doll.

But my fear held me there against the fence. My legs felt trembly and weak. And I had to force myself to breathe as I watched the hole grow larger and larger under the dummy's shoveling hands.

He giggled as he bent over the hole and pulled out the glass case. He whipped his head around once, making sure no one was watching.

I ducked behind the fence and held my breath.

Had he seen me? No.

I raised myself high enough to watch him. He pulled himself quickly to his feet and began brushing dirt off the case with one hand.

In the eerie silver moonlight I could see the doll. I could see its shrunken human head bouncing against the glass bottom as Slappy cleaned the case.

And then, Slappy set the case down gently on the ground and began to pull off the lid.

I gripped the top of the fence so tightly, my hands ached. And suddenly, I heard a voice in my head — *my* voice:

If he gets that doll, he'll wipe your mind clean.

And before I even realized what I was doing, I *leaped* over the fence. And tore through the gravestones.

I tackled Slappy around the waist. I shoved him hard, away from the doll case. And with a burst of strength, I lifted the thrashing, kicking dummy high above my head.

"You're DEAD MEAT, slave!" he screamed. *"You'll be punished for this!"*

And then it was *my* turn to scream.

As a powerful wave of white light blinded me — and wrapped itself around me, trapping me in its beam.

21

I blinked. And blinked again, struggling to fight the light. It divided in two. Two beams of light.

Car headlights!

My eyes slowly adjusted. And I recognized my parents' car.

Dad pushed open the driver's door and slid out. He was in his striped pajamas. "Britney?" he called, shielding his eyes with one hand. "We saw you leave. We followed you. What are you doing here with Ethan's dummy?"

Slappy had gone limp. I still held him above my head.

"Why are you burying Ethan's dummy?" Mom called. She stepped out of the car, wrapping her brown robe around her. "Have you gone *crazy*? Out here in the middle of the night?"

"You know how important that dummy is to Ethan," Dad said. "How could you *bury* it? How could you do such a mean thing?"

"You — you don't understand!" I gasped. "I . . . I'm not burying it. I . . . I . . . I was trying —"

I let out a frustrated cry. "Oh, I can't explain it to you! You wouldn't understand!"

"We have eyes, Britney," Mom said. "We can see the hole you dug. We can see you putting Ethan's dummy into the hole."

Dad motioned for Mom to be quiet. "It's okay," he said softly. He climbed over the fence and started walking toward me, a step at a time.

"It's okay, Brit. Just stay there, sweetie. Don't move. We'll get you to the doctor first thing in the morning. We'll get you the help you need."

"Give Dad the dummy, dear," Mom said. "And come get in the car. We'll take care of you. You know we will."

Lying limp in my hands, Slappy giggled. "You're a big loser," he whispered. "Guess we're going home together — *slave*. I'll come back tomorrow for the doll. Then Slappy wins for good!"

22

I couldn't take that. I couldn't let him win.

My anger exploded in a scream that echoed off the granite tombstones: "NOOOOOOOOOOO!"

I knew what I had to do. I jerked Slappy high over my head — and with all my strength, heaved him headfirst into the glass case.

I heard a deafening *craaaaack* as the glass split. I saw the case shatter under the dummy's hard wooden head.

Slappy uttered a sharp groan as his face slammed into the doll.

Yes! Yesssss!

The dummy's head smashed against the shriveled, green shrunken head. They were nose to nose!

I uttered a cry and staggered back as the doll began to glow.

The shrunken head glowed with a white light. And the doll began to buzz.

Slappy's arms and legs jerked straight out, as if struck by lightning. The dummy's body jolted once. Twice.

Then Slappy collapsed in a lifeless heap on top of the doll case.

I waited . . . waited.

Slappy didn't move.

The Mind Stealer doll had claimed another victim.

I suddenly realized that tears were rolling down my cheeks. My whole body trembled. I took a deep breath and tried to calm myself.

"Britney, what's going on?" Dad asked, stepping up beside me.

"It . . . it's okay," I choked out. "Really. It's all over. No more crazy dummy stories. I promise. It's all over."

Mom stepped up beside me and put her arm around my waist. "I hope you're telling the truth," she said.

"I am," I insisted. "Here." I gathered up the lifeless dummy and handed it to Dad. "Here. Let's take it back to Ethan. Everything will be fine from now on."

"Let's get you back home," Mom said. She started to guide me to the car.

I took a few steps, then remembered the Mind Stealer. "One more thing I have to do," I said. "Go back to the car. I'll be there in one second."

I waited till they began walking to the car. The dummy's arms and legs dangled lifelessly as Dad carried it away.

I was finally breathing normally. I felt so happy . . . so relieved.

Slappy was gone. His mind erased.

Now I just had to deal with the Mind Stealer doll.

I dropped to my knees and stared at it through the cracked lid of the glass case. The dry, black lips were curled in a smile. The empty eye sockets had opened wide.

I forced myself to look away. Carefully, I lifted the case off the ground and lowered it into the hole. Then I began to shove dirt over it, pawing the dirt frantically with both hands.

Breathing hard, I scooped dirt into the hole until the case was completely buried.

Yes! The doll was buried deep under the dirt now. Hidden where it could do no more harm.

I pulled myself to my feet and brushed the dirt off the knees of my jeans. My legs were trembling, my heart pounding.

I took a deep breath. Then I turned and started to walk away.

I walked three or four steps. Then I heard the voice.

Slappy's voice. An ugly, crackling rasp — dry as dead leaves . . . Slappy calling to me from inside the buried doll . . .

"*I'll be back, Britney. I'm a BAAAAAAD boy!*"

ENTER
HORRORLAND

The Invitation

DEAR BRITNEY CROSBY:

Let the SCREAMS begin! You have won a free, weeklong stay at HORRORLAND Theme Park, the SCARIEST Place on Earth!

Bring your PARENTS. Bring your friend MOLLY MOLLOY. And be sure to bring something to feed the WEREWOLVES (like an arm or a leg!).

We've enclosed FREE PASSES to CROCODILE CAFÉ, where you can grab a quick bite. And free tickets to our challenging SWIM—WITH—A—HUNGRY—SHARK ride! (Hope you're a FAST swimmer!)

You don't need a ticket to the BOTTOMLESS QUICKSAND PIT. Drop in anytime!

We know you and Molly will never forget your stay at our famous hotel, STAGGER INN—it's a real SCREAM! (Really!)

So come be our GHOST—oops—we mean GUEST. We look forward to SCARING you!

Please RSVP to:
Di Kwickley, Guest Relations

1

Molly and I sat in the backseat of my parents' car and talked all the way to HorrorLand. After four straight hours of our talk talk talk, Dad cranked up the radio as loud as he could. That was his subtle hint that we should take a break.

"You two are chattering like magpies," Mom said.

"What are magpies?" I asked.

"Little black-and-white birds that chatter a lot," Mom said. "Why don't you two enjoy the scenery for a while?"

"Yeah. For sure," I said.

Molly and I went back to our conversation. We were totally *psyched*.

Our friends Kaitlin and Jason went to HorrorLand last spring. They told us all about it when they got back. They said it was the coolest place they'd ever been.

"They have a werewolf petting zoo," Kaitlin

said. "Do you believe it?" She laughed. "The were-wolves looked totally real! It was awesome!"

Jason liked the rides. He said to be sure to check out the Doom Slide, the world's longest slide. "And don't miss Black Lagoon Water Park," he said. "You'll love the Bottomless Canoe ride, and you won't *believe* Quicksand Beach. Once you start sinking, you think you'll never stop!"

So here we were, on our way to the famous, scary theme park, riding through endless farm-land, all the windows down because the air condi-tioner stopped working, talking nonstop.

Finally, the park came into view. We drove through the wide-open mouth of an enormous purple dragon. It had to be ten stories high! Into the endless parking lot, jammed with cars.

Up ahead, I saw a tall green-and-purple bill-board. It said:

WELCOME TO HORRORLAND.
Where Nightmares Come to Life!

I slapped Molly a high five. "This is gonna be awesome!" I cried.

"And it's all *free*!" Dad chimed in. "Britney, what did you do to win free tickets?"

I shrugged. "Beats me. I didn't enter a contest or anything. I don't know *how* I got picked."

"They seemed to know a lot about us," Molly said. "They knew my name. It's totally weird."

"This is one of the biggest theme parks in the world," Dad said. "They do a lot of research on people."

We climbed out of the car. The afternoon sun beamed down from a clear, cloudless sky. Large black birds circled high overhead.

"Are those buzzards?" Mom asked, shielding her eyes with one hand. "Don't buzzards feed on dead things?"

Dad laughed. "They're probably animated robots or something. Very clever."

He watched the buzzards for a moment. Then he popped the trunk and started to pull out our bags.

I tried to see into the park. But it was surrounded by a tall green fence.

Deep, scary organ music poured out of speakers above our heads.

Mom frowned. "That's the kind of music they play at funerals," she murmured.

Molly tugged the sleeve of my T-shirt. "Hear those kids screaming?" she asked. She suddenly looked frightened.

Yes. I heard loud screams on the other side of the fence. "Sounds like they're on a roller coaster or something," I told her. "Remember? Jason said the rides here are *incredible*."

Dad pulled out his new digital camera and snapped some pictures of the park entrance and the big WELCOME sign. Then we carried our bags down the long row of cars. I spotted a ticket booth next to the wide iron front gate. It looked like a little castle and was green and purple like everything else at HorrorLand.

Molly laughed. "Check out that sign." She pointed to the fence beside the ticket booth.

The sign read: YOU MUST BE THIS TALL TO ENTER. And the arrow was only two feet off the ground!

Dad pulled out his camera and clicked a photo of it.

"Looks like fun," Mom said. "It'll be like living inside a horror movie for a week."

We lined our bags up on the walk and stepped up to the ticket window.

No one in there.

"That's weird," Dad said. "Maybe this booth is closed."

"It can't be," I said. "Look around. It's the only ticket booth."

"Be patient," Mom said. "Someone will come."

So we waited. And waited some more. With the hot sun broiling us, sweat making the back of my neck prickle. Listening to the screams inside and watching the fat buzzards swoop low overhead.

"Something is wrong," Dad muttered. "If this is the only ticket booth, I think —"

He never finished his sentence.

Suddenly, a hideous horned creature — purple

and green with pointed fangs and giant curled claws — leaped out through the ticket window. With a low, nasty growl, it wrapped its claws around my throat.

And I started to scream.

"Sorry," the creature said. He let go of my throat and patted my shoulder gently. "Just doing my job, you know." He had a British accent.

We all laughed. My heart was still pounding. But I didn't want to let on that he had scared me.

He climbed back into the ticket booth and poked his head out the opening. His long horns scraped the sides of the booth.

"I'm a Horror," he said. "We're the park workers. You know. The guides. It's not a bad job. I have paid vacations — and I get to *eat* any small children I can catch."

We all laughed.

On the other side of the fence, I heard snarling animal sounds. The snarls turned to a roar. And then I heard people running and screaming their heads off.

The Horror shook his head. "Sounds like one of the creatures escaped Werewolf Village," he said. "That happens from time to time. It can be very messy."

Molly and I exchanged glances. I wished Molly would lighten up. She looked so tense. She *had* to know this was all a joke.

"We have a special invitation," Dad said. He pulled the letter from his wallet and handed it to the Horror.

The Horror pretended to eat it. Then he pulled it out of his mouth and read it carefully. He punched some keys on his computer and then poked his head back out.

"Yes, I see," he said, suddenly serious. "I see. Britney and Molly, you are *very special* guests." Then he laughed a cold and evil laugh.

His laugh gave me a chill. What did he mean by *very special*?

"So, do we just go in?" Dad asked.

The Horror shook his head. Once again, his pointy horns scraped the walls of the booth. "No, you can't go in," he said.

Dad squinted at him. "I . . . don't understand."

"Before I can let you in," the Horror said, "I have to make each one of you scream."

I laughed. "You're joking, right? We all have to scream?"

"We keep your scream on file," he said. "So we can identify you later."

Excuse me?

Identify us later?

What did *that* mean?

The Horror pulled out a small black microphone. "Whenever you're ready," he said. "It's connected to my computer."

We lined up one by one and did our best scream into the microphone. Mom's was the best. I couldn't believe it. She really sounded like she was in a horror movie.

Molly did a tiny, shrill scream. You could barely hear her. Mine was pretty good. Maybe too long. I screamed till my throat hurt.

After Dad screamed, his face turned bright red. He's kind of shy and I think he was embarrassed.

The metal gate swung open. The Horror pointed inside. "Wait by the road there. A taxi will pick you up and take you to the hotel. A Horror will be waiting to take you to your rooms."

The four of us walked through the tall gate. It slid shut behind us and clicked, as if locking us inside.

Dad suddenly turned. "Hey, wait —" he called to the Horror. "Our suitcases."

The Horror stepped out of the ticket booth and walked over to our bags. "You won't be needing these where *you're* going!" he said.

He pulled a blowtorch from behind his back, flamed it up — and set our suitcases on fire!

3

"Hey, stop —!" Dad screamed. "What are you *doing*?"

I stood there, frozen in shock. Molly squeezed my hand.

Mom and Dad both grabbed the bars of the metal gate and tried to slide it open. But it had snapped shut. We were trapped inside.

Flames rose high over the suitcases. The cases burned like paper, turning brown, then black under the darting flames.

"Are you *crazy*? You can't do that!" Dad screamed. "All our belongings! Everything we brought!" He tugged at the bars.

I peered through the gate. The Horror had vanished.

"Calm down," Mom said, holding on to his shoulder. "Come on, Sean. Calm down. It *has* to be a joke."

"Right," I said. "It's special effects, Dad. Don't lose it. We just got here. Bet you a million dollars our bags will be at the hotel when we get there."

The four of us gazed through the bars. Our cases were black and charred. Flames burned over our clothes, making a sizzling, crackling sound.

I spun around when I heard a horn honk. A long yellow taxi squealed to a stop beside us. In big black letters on the side, it read: LAST RIDE CAB CO.

A Horror stuck his head out of the driver's window. "Crosby family? Ready for your *last ride*? All aboard!" he called. He had a high, scratchy voice. He reached back and pulled open the back door for us.

All four of us squeezed into the backseat. The brown leather was cracked and faded. The car smelled kind of sour.

"Buckle up!" the Horror said, making the engine roar.

We all reached behind us. "There aren't any seat belts," Molly said.

"No problem," the Horror muttered. "I've got *mine* buckled."

"Is it a long ride?" Dad asked.

"I know a shortcut," he said.

The taxi lurched forward. Molly grabbed my arm. As we picked up speed, I stared out at the park. It rolled by so fast, it was mostly a blur of bright colors and faces.

I saw some kids running from a giant, roaring gorilla. And we passed under a ride where kids were sitting on huge bats, their wings flapping as they circled the sky.

A red-and-black sign on the front of a very tall building read: VAMPIRE STATE BUILDING. BLOOD DONORS WELCOME. Across the road, I glimpsed a tiny shack with a sign out front: WORM AND BAIT SHOP. ALL YOU CAN EAT.

We passed a crowded outdoor theater. Outside, a sign read: TV'S HIT SHOW — DANCING WITH THE SQUIDS. Squinting out the window, I saw three kids onstage wrestling with giant squids *twice* their size!

"Can we skip that one?" Molly asked.

"It's a lot of fun," the driver said. "Unless they *sit* on you."

He slowed the taxi as we swerved through a crowd of kids in Scout uniforms. "Don't want to mow down too many Scouts," he said in his scratchy voice. "They complain if I hit more than two or three of them!"

The road got narrow and bumpy as we entered what looked like a swamp with tangled palm trees and tall ferns. The car zoomed forward and my head hit the roof with each hard bump.

"Ow. Could you slow down a little?" Mom asked.

The driver didn't answer. His eyes were on the controls. He spun the wheel one way, then the other.

The taxi bumped off the road, into tall grass.

109

The tires slid and spun in the mud. The Horror yanked the wheel from side to side. He pumped hard on the brakes again and again.

"It's busted! I *knew* this would happen!" he cried. "I warned them at the garage."

"OWWW!" I yelled as we hit a deep hole. Ferns and tree branches smacked the windows as we sped over the marshy grass.

"This is no joke!" the Horror cried. "Look!" He spun the wheel completely around.

"What's wrong?" Dad cried.

"The steering and the brakes are out!" the Horror said. "I can't control this thing!"

We bumped over something hard. The car jerked up, then down again. We picked up speed. It was all a green blur outside the window.

"This isn't part of the deal," the Horror said. "They promised they'd fix it!"

He pumped the brakes a few more times, but the car roared ahead.

"I'm really sorry, folks. This never happened before," he said. "I . . . I'm really sorry to do this."

I cried out as he shoved open his door. He let go of the steering wheel, turned his body. And — screaming his head off — dove from the car.

I saw him tumble through the tall grass. His open car door scraped against thick vines and tree limbs as we roared past. Faster — bumping and lurching. The four of us bounced with every bump, helpless in the backseat, unable to reach the controls.

Then I saw the red brick wall rise up in front of us.

I opened my mouth to scream.

But Molly beat me to it. "We — we're going to HIT IT!" she wailed. "We're going to CRASH!"

4

"*YAAAAAIIIIIIII!*"

All four of us screamed in horror.

As the brick wall rose up in front of us, the taxi squealed to a sudden stop. My head bumped the car roof again. I looked down and saw I was squeezing Molly's hand.

Our doors popped open. No one moved. I sat there shaking, struggling to catch my breath.

The driver came trotting up to us. He reached in, took my arm, and helped pull me from the car. "Hope you enjoyed the ride," he said. His yellow eyes twinkled.

"Huh?" I gasped. "Enjoy —?"

He reached in to help Molly out, too. Mom and Dad scrambled out the other door, shaking their heads, massaging their shoulders, and blinking hard.

"One of these days, I've *got* to get a driver's license!" the Horror said. "This happens to me every trip!"

He pointed to the ground.

And we all saw the metal tracks under the taxi tires. "The car isn't real. It runs on tracks!" I said.

The Horror nodded. "You got *that* right. I don't really drive it." He rubbed his shoulder. "The hardest part of *my* job is diving out of a speeding car twenty times a day!"

He shut all the doors, then climbed back behind the wheel. "Follow the path to your hotel!" he shouted. "And if you need a ride, you know who to call!" Then the car turned around and rolled away.

I hugged Molly and laughed. We all started talking at once. That driver had us all fooled.

"From now on, I'm not going to believe *anything*!" I said. "From now on, I'm going to remember that everything here is a total fake!"

Famous last words?

Yes. You got *that* right.

5

We followed the path and found ourselves in a wide, round plaza. Crowds of kids and families walked around the big circle, visiting the shops, food carts, arcades, and rides.

A green-and-purple Horror stood on a platform, juggling three skulls.

"Are they real?" a little girl asked.

The Horror held one up. "Yeah. This is my uncle Tony."

Everyone laughed.

An arrow sign read: HAUNTED THEATER. Another sign pointed to Good-bye Land: MAKE IT YOUR LAST STOP — ON EARTH!

Next to it, a green-and-purple sign read: WELCOME TO ZOMBIE PLAZA. WE HOPE YOU SHOP TILL YOU DROP.

"This is awesome!" I declared. "What should we do first?"

"First, we should check in," Dad said. He shielded

his eyes with one hand. "Where is that guide to take us to the hotel?"

"Why do we have to check in right away?" Mom asked. "Let's have some fun first."

"Yeah. Fun!" I agreed. "I vote for fun first!"

"Me, too," Molly said.

Dad shrugged. "Okay, okay. I just want to see if our bags arrived safely."

If you haven't guessed it, let me tell you. My dad is a total worrywart. Even on vacation. *Especially* on vacation!

Mom wiped her forehead. "That crazy taxi ride made my throat so dry. Can we get some ice cream?" She pointed to the green-and-purple cart across the plaza.

We dodged three teenagers chasing one another with long swords and trotted over to it. It wasn't an ice-cream cart. The sign read: FROZEN EYEBALLS ON A STICK.

"Yuck," Molly groaned.

A Horror in a stained yellow apron leaned on the cart with an ice-cream scoop in one hand. "Do you want plain or bloodshot?" he asked.

We ordered four plain, and they tasted a lot like vanilla ice cream. As we licked our eyeballs, we walked around Zombie Plaza.

"Dad, do you have a token?" I asked. I pulled him over to an old-fashioned-looking fortune-teller's booth. MADAME DOOM SEES ALL, the sign announced. Behind the glass sat a wooden dummy of an old woman in a red velvet dress and a matching turban.

Dad handed me a shiny HorrorLand token, and I dropped it in the slot. "I love these things," I said.

I watched Madame Doom creak to life. Her wooden hand slowly moved over a stack of little cards and pushed one out at me.

"What does it say?" Molly asked, bumping up beside me. "What's your future?"

I gazed at the card. Blank. I turned it over. Blank on the other side, too.

"Hey, I got cheated," I said.

And then Madame Doom's mouth moved up and down, and in a creaky voice, she said: *You don't have a future, Britney.*

"Huh?" I stared at the old woman, waiting for her to say more. But the dummy froze and stared blankly straight ahead.

"Another HorrorLand joke," Mom said. "I'll bet you anything that *all* of her cards are blank."

"But how did she know my name?" I asked.

No one heard me. They'd all moved on to a store called MAKE A FACE! The front window was filled with rubber masks. "Those don't look like Halloween masks," Molly said. "The faces are like . . . like real kids! And why do they all look like they're *screaming*?"

I followed her inside. Molly and I tried on some

116

totally hairy monster masks. The hair felt like real hair. And the skin was *warm*. The masks clung to our faces. We had trouble pulling them off.

"This is *so* creeping me out," Molly said. "Let's move on."

"No, check this out," I said. I pulled her into the next room. The walls were covered with rubber masks of human faces. Mostly kids.

"Each one is different," Molly said. "They must be handmade. The kids all look so pale and sad. And . . ."

She stopped and followed my gaze. We both stared at the two masks in a display case on the back counter. Two girls with coppery hair.

"Molly," I whispered. "It's . . . US!"

A Horror stepped up behind the counter. She had long black hair tied in a ponytail, and pale yellow eyes. She turned to the two masks. "They *do* look a little like you," she said. "How odd!"

She started to pull one off its hook. "Want to try them on? They're brand-new. I just got them a few minutes ago."

Molly backed away. "Uh . . . no thanks," she stammered.

"But it looks so much like you," the Horror said. "You could take it home and totally freak your friends."

She held it out to me. "Try it on, Britney. Once it's on, you won't want to take it off."

"Well . . ."

"Girls, we have to go," Dad said, stepping up behind us. "I really think we should check into the hotel."

Molly and I turned and started to follow Mom

and Dad out of the store. "Maybe later," I called to the Horror.

We stepped out onto the plaza. "Whoa. *She* knew my name, too!" I said. "What's up with that?"

"Hey — check it out!" Dad pointed to a tall stone building across the plaza. It looked like an old castle with two towers and a thick blanket of ivy growing down the side. As we made our way toward it, we could see the sign on the front awning: STAGGER INN.

"Must be our hotel," Dad said.

A Horror came running up to us. His purple cape fluttered in the air as he ran. He kept straightening the horns on top of his head with one hand.

"Hi, I'm Sean Crosby," Dad said. "We were looking for you."

The Horror glanced behind him. "Quick — listen to me!" he said in a hoarse whisper.

He glanced back again. "They might be watching me," he said breathlessly. "Some of us don't like what's happening here. Some of us are trying to stop it."

He grabbed my dad's shirtsleeve. "Get *out* of the park!" he cried. "As fast as you can. Get *out* of here!"

7

The Horror dropped Dad's arm. Then he tucked something into my hand — and took off, running full speed across the plaza.

The four of us watched him openmouthed. Then we burst out laughing.

"He's a good actor," Molly said. "For a second, I totally believed him."

"Guess they'll do *anything* to scare you here," Mom said.

"Look, he left me a note or something," I said. I pulled it out of my palm and unfolded it. Squinting at the scrawled writing, I read it out loud:

"*Find the other park.*"

"The other park?" Molly said. "*Where?* What does that mean?"

Another Horror came walking up to us. She had long blond hair flowing back between her curled horns. She wore purple tights under a short, straight green skirt.

"Welcome to the scariest place on earth," she said, then laughed. "My name is Druella. Y'all look scared already! That's a good thing!"

She smiled at us. "You're Britney and Molly, right?" she asked. "Very special guests. Follow me." She swung her cape behind her and led us into the hotel.

A Horror at the front desk was filing his claws with a long nail file. He didn't look up as we passed.

We walked through the front lobby. There were chairs and couches all around — and a skeleton sprawled in each one! The walls were covered with huge oil paintings, all of children screaming their heads off. A headless man played scary music on an organ in the corner.

"This is the place to relax," Druella said.

She led us into the narrow elevator. When the doors rattled shut, it was pitch-black inside. The elevator groaned, then slowly began to move.

She showed my parents to Room 202 on the second floor. "Are the girls next door?" Mom asked.

Druella shook her head. "No. They're coming with me. Our special guests all stay on the thirteenth floor."

Naturally.

Back into the dark elevator. It creaked and groaned and seemed to take forever to climb to 13.

Druella led us down a dark, winding hall to

Room 1313. She handed me a key card. "You don't mind that this room is haunted — do you?" she said.

Molly and I laughed. "Of course not," I said.

"Don't be scared," Druella whispered. "The ghost only comes out in the day and in the night." She turned and started back down the hall. "If you need anything, just SCREAM!" she called.

I inserted the key card and the heavy door creaked open. A blast of cold air greeted us. The air conditioner must have been turned on full blast.

I fumbled in the darkness for the light switch and clicked on the lights.

"Wow! Check it out. It's totally awesome!" Molly cried. "Look at that enormous flat-screen TV."

The room was almost as big as my house! We had a small kitchen, and a dining room, and a long couch in front of the immense TV, and two twin beds with at least a dozen pillows each.

I jumped onto a bed and bounced up and down. "Soft!" I said, sinking into the pillows. "This has got to be the greatest room ever!"

"I thought it would look like a dungeon or something," Molly said. "But it isn't scary at all."

"And check this out," I said. I picked up a handful of green-and-purple-wrapped candy bars from the bed table. They were called Shock-A-Lot Bars. I tossed one to Molly. "Free candy!"

We sat on the edge of the bed and devoured a couple of candy bars.

Molly wiped chocolate off her chin with the back of her hand. Her smile faded. "Our suitcases," she murmured. "They're not here."

I jumped up. "Maybe in the closet?"

I crossed the room and pulled open the closet door. "Molly — I don't believe this!" I exclaimed. "The closet is twice as big as the one in my room back home — and it's filled with clothes!"

Molly hurried over. We began pawing through the racks of designer jeans and skirts and awesome T-shirts and tops.

"All in our sizes!" Molly said. "Weird!"

We tried on a few outfits. I laughed. "I hope they really did burn my old clothes. This stuff is way cooler."

Molly stopped suddenly and stared at me. "You must *really* be a special guest, Brit. And you don't have a clue how you won all this?"

"Not a clue," I said. I slipped into a red-and-yellow sundress. I spun around the room. "Hey — no mirror."

"Huh?" Molly had pulled on a pair of white shorts and a pale green T-shirt. She walked into the closet. "No mirror in here, either. Weird. All these fabulous clothes to try on — and not a single mirror in the room."

"Let's go show off our new outfits to my parents," I said.

"Okay, but we should hurry. We should get back out in the park before the sun goes down," Molly said. "Maybe check out Werewolf Village. Kaitlin said it was totally not to be believed."

I was glad to see Molly finally getting into it. I locked the door and tucked the key card in my pocket. Then we walked down the long, winding hall to the elevator.

The elevator doors scraped open. We stepped inside. The doors closed, leaving us in total darkness. The elevator creaked as it slowly started to go down.

Molly grabbed my arm. "Why can't they put a light in the elevator?"

I laughed. "Hel-lo. How scary would *that* be?"

The elevator bumped hard. Then it stopped. The door didn't open.

We waited in silence for a while, but it didn't start up again.

"I . . . I think we're stuck between floors," Molly whispered.

Before I could say anything, the elevator bumped again and started to scrape its way down. "Another joke," I muttered. "They really do know how to scare us — don't they?"

The door slid open on the second floor. We stepped out into the dimly lit hallway and followed it to my parents' room — number 202.

I raised my hand to knock — then stopped.

"That's weird," I said. The door was open a crack. "My dad is a nut about always closing doors."

I pushed it open and called out: "Mom? Dad?"

No answer.

Molly and I stepped into the room. "Hey, Mom? Hey —"

My eyes darted around the room. Empty.

I checked the bathroom. "Mom? Dad?"

No sign that anyone had been here.

I turned to Molly. "Where *are* they?"

"This room is kind of small and dark," I said. "They probably changed rooms."

Molly chewed her bottom lip. "But why didn't they call and tell us?"

I shrugged. "Come on. We'll ask at the front desk."

We took the stairs. We didn't want to get back in that elevator.

A Horror sat behind the desk. He was reading a paperback book called *Die, Monster, Die.* He looked up when Molly and I charged up to him.

"Have you seen my parents?" I asked breathlessly. "Mr. and Mrs. Crosby? They were in 202, but —"

He tapped on his keyboard and then squinted at the monitor. "Crosby? Oh, right," he said. "They checked out a few minutes ago."

"Huh?" I cried. "No way. That's impossible." I leaned over the counter, trying to read the screen. "Please — check again."

"I definitely checked them out," the Horror said. "They said they couldn't wait to get home."

He squinted at the monitor. "Crosby — right?"

I nodded. "Yeah. Crosby."

"They're gone," he said. "They split."

My mouth dropped open. "But — but they wouldn't leave without us. That's crazy!"

The Horror shrugged. "Go figure."

I heard footsteps on the marble floor. A family came hurrying up to the front desk — two smiling parents and a little boy with chocolate smeared on his face.

"We're the Hopper family," the father told the Horror. "Is this where we check in?"

The Horror tapped some keys on his keyboard. He frowned. "We're pretty full. Do you mind sleeping in the dungeon for a few nights? The torture rack is pretty comfortable."

I pulled Molly off to the side. "I get it!" I said. "I don't think we should worry about my parents. It *has* to be one of the Horrors' scary jokes. They *love* scaring us every minute."

Molly squinted at me. "Do you really think it's just a joke? Maybe we should check your parents' room one more time."

"All right," I said.

We took the stairs. The door to room 202 was half open. I guess we left it that way. I pushed it open all the way, and we stepped inside.

I kind of expected Mom and Dad to be there this time. But the room was still empty.

I started to look around. Something on the floor caught my eye. I picked it up and examined it.

"A camera?" Molly said.

"My dad's digital camera," I murmured, turning it in my hands. "It's . . . still on."

"Your dad wouldn't leave without his camera," Molly said. She bit her bottom lip. I could see she was really tense.

"Maybe he left it here for us," Molly said. "Maybe he took a picture with it. You know. As a clue. To let us know where they went."

"Yeah. Maybe," I said. I could feel myself getting excited. "Maybe."

I pressed a button on the back. And instantly, a picture came up on the view screen.

I held it up to my face, and we both stared at it.

"N-no!" I stammered. "It . . . *can't* be!"

The photo was a little blurred. But I could see the figure clearly . . . the grinning figure standing right here in this hotel room.

It was SLAPPY!

To be continued in . . .

#2 CREEP FROM THE DEEP

About the Author

R.L. Stine's books are read all over the world. So far, his books have sold more than 300 million copies, making him one of the most popular children's authors in history. Besides Goosebumps, R.L. Stine has written the teen series Fear Street and the funny series Rotten School, as well as the Mostly Ghostly series, The Nightmare Room series, and the two-book thriller *Dangerous Girls*. R.L. Stine lives in New York with his wife, Jane, and Minnie, his King Charles spaniel. You can learn more about him at www.RLStine.com.

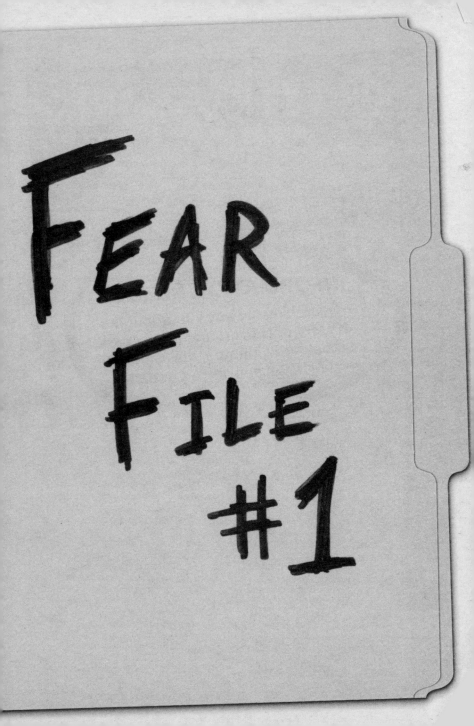

INFORMATION NEEDED

Searching for any info about the
history of HorrorLand theme park.
Postcards, photos, etc. Contact:
LM1@EscapeHorrorLand.com

STAGGER INN

Doom Service Menu

Chef Gurgitate's Proud Motto: "EAT OR BE EATEN!"
(Please note: the kitchen is closed from midnight to 6 a.m. for daily repairs and rounding up of escaped ingredients.)

BREAKFAST

CEREAL......$5
Your choice of Mice Crispies, Dirt Loops, Yucky Charms, or Cinnamon Scabs (now with more scabs!).

FRUIT BAT SALAD......$4
No one can make a salad out of a fruit bat like Chef Gurgitate. Served with tangy animal thingies.

THE YOLK'S ON YOU!......$6
A different egg dish every morning—and it's so easy to pick out the bones!

SQUEEZINGS......$10
Start your day with a tall stack of the chef's famous squeezings, collected from around the park.

FIND THE REST at
WWW.ESCAPEHorrorLAND.COM
SIGNED,
LM1

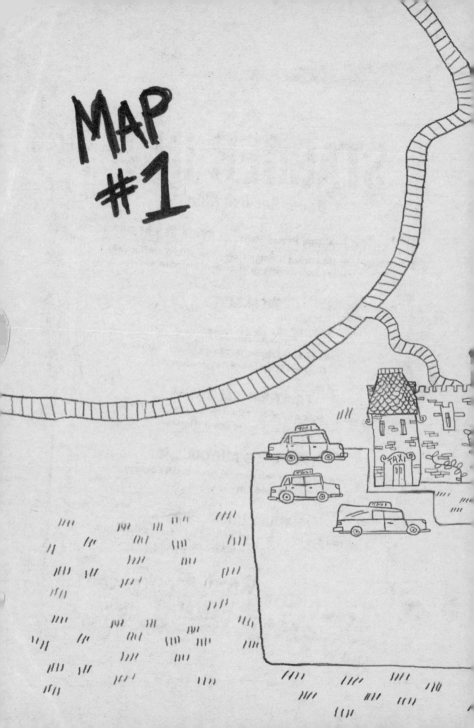

NOW A MAJOR
MOTION PICTURE

JACK BLACK

Goosebumps